JN134696

神のくちづけ

合田 和厚

The Kiss of God

Yasuhiro Goda

光は空を成し　空の狭間は時となる

光が愛ならば　時空は愛の軌跡
そう宇宙は愛という旅をする

あなたがこの宇宙の彼方　138億光年先の光の中に
宇宙の始まりを見るように

あなたが死んでも　1000光年先の星には
生まれたばかりのあなたを見る者がいる
あなたが逝った何億光年のちにも　この宇宙には
あなたを見る誰かがいる

この星からあなたが消え去っても
あなたの姿は光に乗り
この宇宙のある限り永遠に生き続ける

万物は死して消え去れど
その一生はこの宇宙の終焉まで
光という愛のスクリーンの中で輝き続ける

神はそれを見続けている

あなたの生命は　神の愛そのもの

Light forms the skies and between the skies resides time

If light is love, space-time is the trajectory of love
The universe does indeed take a journey of love

You can see the beginning of the universe in the light 13.8 billion light years away

Likewise, when you die, someone on a star 1,000 light years away watches your birth
Hundreds of millions of light years after you pass away, someone in this universe will watch you

Even after you disappear from this planet
Carried by light, your image will live on eternally as long as this universe continues

Although all beings die and disappear
Their entire lives continue to shine in the screen of love called light until this universe ends

God will continue to watch over it

Your life is indeed God's love

目次　*Contents*

CHAPTER 5

永遠の終結と始まりの章

EPILOGUE

難解なるものの儚くも美しい真理の章

PROLOGUE

夢とまどろみの章

DREAMING AND DROWSING

自由ならくがき

夢みる時

そっと振り返る

幼き日々の微笑みを

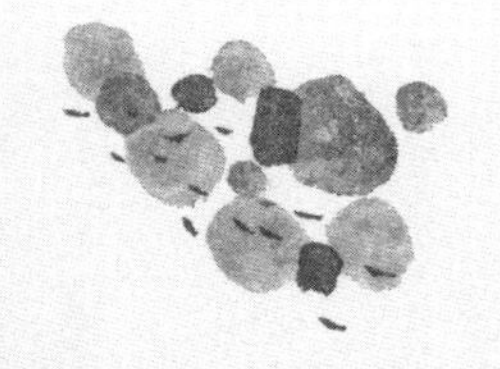

夢　*PROOF*

夢みることは　簡単だと　僕がいう
夢みることができる人は　幸せだと　あなたがいう

悲しみの中でも
夢みることができるなら
やがて
悲しみは去りゆくだろう
けれど
夢みることも忘れ
この場所から一歩も踏み出せないでいるとき
あなたは　どうすればいいのだろう

陽は昇り　風は吹き　雲は流れ　時は去り

星の煌めきの中で
静寂さえも美しく輝き始める

あなたが涙にくれるこの時にも　自然は語りかけている

夢みることは簡単だと
その素直な心で　ありのままを見ればいいと

自然の調べは　神の吐息のように
そっと優しくあなたを包みこむ

無限なるほど広大な宇宙の息吹きに抱かれ
あなたは息をしている

あなたが悲しんでいるということ
それは
あなたが生きているという証し
そしてそれは
いつの日か　あなたが神のすぐ傍にいたと　思い出すことのできる証し

悲しみの涙に、濡れたその素直な心で　夢みることができるなら

目 *DESIRE*

若かった頃
外の世界ばかりに
目がいっていた

父の事も
母の事も
真剣に考えたことがなかった

自分の傍らにいた人や
手に入れたものを
大切に慈しむ事もなかった

心はいつも好奇心に溢れ
新鮮な驚きを
求めていた

近視に
遠くのも
てしまうのも
近くのものが見え
まうのもきっとあな
いるせいなのです
少し変えるだけ
くるのです
心の窓と
です

年老いてから

身のまわりの世界にだけ

目がいくようになった

息子の事や

娘の事ばかり

真剣に考えている

自分の夢や欲望を

真面目にかなえようと

することもなくなった

心は常に乱されるのを嫌い

外からくる変化を

拒絶するようになった

なって

のがボヤケ

遠視になって

づらくなってし

たの欲望が偏って

心の視点をほんの

で視力は戻って

だって目は

いうぐらい

から

満月　*DARKNESS*

一点の陰りもない
満月の輝き　美しくも神々しく
さえある完璧な月の姿を目にして　人々は
それを名月と呼ぶ　けれど満月の強い輝きは　天の
川や他の星座の輝きを消し去ってしまう 半月を美し
いと思う夜もある　三日月を美しいと思う夜もある 新月
の真っ暗な夜空に浮かぶ無数の星の瞬きを美しいと思う夜
もある 長くて短い君の人生において　栄光に何ひとつ不安
を抱かぬ夜　満月のように光り輝く君は優しさを忘れ去って
しまうだろう　いつしか愛する人とめぐり逢い　その人の幸
せを君の幸せとする夜 その人の悲しみを君の悲しみと
する夜 君は半月のように心の中にもうひとつの心
を持つ　やがて愛しい子供が生れる夜 君
はその子の為なら犠牲をいとわ
ぬ心を知るだろう

君の心は
三日月のよう
に家族を支える
礎となる　そし
て君がこの世から
去ってしまう夜　君は
夜空に無数の星の瞬
きがあることを知るだ
ろう　君の心は新月
のように姿なくとも
存在する　ただ君
は静かに世界を見
ている　再び神の
光が君を照ら
す時まで

碧　*TIME FOR ME*

夜の終り
朝の始まり

そんな
束の間の時

月の煌めきもなく
太陽の輝きもなく

水平線は消え
空と海が碧くひとつになる時

宇宙のうたたね
静かな吐息

私だけの時間
貴方を想う

別離のあと
嬉びと悲しみの終焉

時間にさえ
取り残されたような時

涙も忘れ
笑顔も忘れ

人生の記憶は消え
過去と未来が碧くひとつになる時

愛のうたたね
静かな風の音

私だけの時間
貴方を想う

美しい星　*FOREVER*

夜の終わりに　降り始めた雪が
悲しみを冷たい時間(とき)の中に　閉じ込めていった
こぼれる涙は　厚い氷の小さな雫となり
夜空の彼方には　もうひとつの涙が流れて消えた

長い時をかけて逢いに来た
動き出す風の場所と
静止した風の場所
悲しみの中に静けさが宿るその瞳の奥に　深い優しさがある

いつからか動き始めた時間(とき)の中で
私は悲しみの数だけ　あなたから遠ざかり
嬉びの数だけ　あなたを遠ざけていった
なのに今
星の瞬く音が聴こえるように
あなたの心の鼓動が聴こえる
風の舞う姿が見えるように
あなたの心の輝きが見える

あなたの優しさは　あなたの悲しみから生まれ
その涙は　夜空に散らばる星となった
あなたは知っている
星の生まれる場所と
星の降り落ちる場所を

あなたの涙が　夜空いっぱいになった時
優しさは満ちあふれ
満天の星の光は降りそそぐ陽のように
長い夜に終わりを告げた

あなたの悲しみは　あの静止した風の場所のせい
あなたの嬉びは　今、動き出す風と共にある
あなたの暖かな涙が　あの凍りついた雪を溶かし
時間（とき）は風に触れ空を舞い　私のそばに微笑むあなたがいる

愛しさの中にある切なさは
別離の訪れを知っているから
ふたりの時間（とき）が　朝焼けの星のように消えていく

生の数だけの死があるように
愛の数だけの悲しみがある
だけど　私は忘れはしない
あなたと逢えた永遠の中のほんのつかの間の時間（とき）
動かぬ時間さえ風に変えた　あなたの優しさが教えてくれたから
心を愛すれば全てが心になり愛だけになる、と

愛しい人よ
あなたと巡り逢えた嬉びは
永遠の夜空に　いつまでも輝き続ける美しい星となる

CHAPTER 1

愛の影の悲しみの章

THE SADNESS OF LOVE'S SHADOW

人はなぜ恋するのか

愛は他者に捧げるもの
恋は我が身に捧げるもの
永遠の中の
限られた時間の中で
僕達は待ちわびている
愛する人にめぐり逢える嬉びを

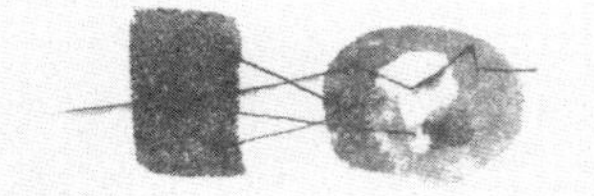

窓辺のバラ　*MYSELF*

恋する男がいた
野に咲くバラがあまりにも美しかったから
彼はそのバラの花を一本つみとって　恋する女に差し出した
彼女は微笑んだ
「なんて美しいバラの花なの」
その日から、彼は彼女に逢うたびに　バラの花をつみとり続けた
何日かたつと、彼女は嬉びの言葉ひとつ　口にしなくなった
彼はそれでも　あの日の彼女の笑顔が忘れられず、バラの花を手渡し続けた
いつの日か、
彼女の部屋の片隅でゴミクズのように萎れていたバラの束を見つけたとき
彼は尋ねた
それには　とても勇気がいったが
「もうバラの花は嫌いになったのかい？」
「…………」
彼女は　なにも答えなかった
答えられなかったのではなく、答えたくなかったのかもしれない
彼は部屋から出ると、黙ってドアを閉めた
帰り道、風にそよぐ野原のバラを見たとき
彼はなにかをひとつ失くし、大切ななにかをひとつ得たような気がした

恋する女がいた
野に咲くバラがあまりにも美しかったから
彼女はそのバラの花を一本つみとり　窓辺に飾った
男は窓辺のバラに気づくこともなく　彼女を抱きよせた
それでも彼女は、彼が訪れるたびバラの花を飾り続けた
いつの日からか、彼女の部屋からバラの花が消えていた
男は彼女のもとに来なくなっていた
彼女は自分の心に尋ねた
それには　とても勇気がいったが
「もう私のことを嫌いになったのかしら？」
「…………」
自らの問いに　彼女は　なにも答えなかった
答えられなかったのではなく、答えたくなかったのかもしれない
彼女は窓辺に腰掛け、野原を見た
もうバラの花は　何処にも咲いていなかった。
彼女は季節が移り変わっていたことさえ忘れていた。
彼女はなにかをひとつ失くし、大切ななにかをひとつ得たような気がした

もうひとりの彼女　*LOVE MYSELF*

恋した時
彼女の中に「もうひとりの彼女」がいた
恋した時
彼の中に「もうひとりの彼」がいた

彼女は「もうひとりの彼女」を愛するために
「もうひとりの彼」を愛した

しかし　彼女は　そのことに気づかなかった

その愛は　自分自身に向けられ
その恋は　そのために必要なものだった

彼に恋したのは　自分自身を愛するためだったから

恋は彼女にとって大切なものだったが
彼にとって彼女の恋は　愛ではなかった

　　彼が去って行った時　彼女は泣いた
　　けれど　その涙が何処から来るものか考えようとはしなかった

彼女の心にあるのは　孤独という苦しみだけだった

彼女の中の 「もうひとりの彼女」が消え
自分自身に戻っただけなのに

　彼女はそれを知らない
　ただ　彼がいなくなった絶望に打ちひしがれている

彼女が嬉びを分かち合っていたのは
彼とではなく 「もうひとりの彼女」とだった

彼女が苦しみを分かち合っていたのも
彼とではなく 「もうひとりの彼女」とだった

彼女が語りかけていたのは　彼でなく自分自身だったのだ

　だから　彼女は嫉妬深く彼を束縛し　不満の全てを彼の責任にした
　自分自身を愛するために　彼を苦しめるのに何の疑問も抱かなかった

彼を自由に操ることが　彼女の恋の成就だった
彼を自分の影とすることが　彼女の恋の目的だった

自分自身を愛せないもどかしさが　恋という名の呪縛をつくり
その恋は　他の誰かに自分自身を愛させる道具となった

自己愛とは　自らを愛せない彼女の言葉

自らを愛せない不安と恐れが作りだす恋に　本当の愛は生まれはしない
なぜなら　恋も愛のひとつなのだから

神のくちづけ　*THE REASON OF FALLING IN LOVE*

女は我知らず
恋する男に神の幻影を見る
心すべてを開き　躰すべてを預ける
時には甘え　時には泣き　時にはすがる

誰にも言えない事も
誰にも見せない事も
恋する男の前では　素直な女となる

神に捧げるように
身も心も恋する男のためにある

男は我知らず
恋する女に神の幻影を見る
心すべてを開き　躰すべてで愛する
時には甘え　時には怖れ　時にはすがる

誰にも言えない事も
誰にも見せない事も
恋する女の前では　正直な男となる

神に捧げるように
身も心も恋する女のためにある

神に出逢えぬため
神を我がものとしたいため
男と女は恋をする

めぐり逢えぬ神への憧憬が　人の心に恋を生む

恋する女のために
恋する男のために
誰しも一度は神の似姿となる
けれど
ただの人間へと戻っていく

恋する男の中に
恋する女の中に
誰しも一度は神の愛を見る
なのに
ただの人間だと気づいていく

恋多き女よ
恋多き男よ
神を求める者よ　そして神と求められる者よ

せめて
くちづけを交わすその時に　神の幻影となれるなら
無の心で慕う神のように　いつまでも

恋愛　*FLOWER OF LOVE*

愛されない辛さは
愛することのできない辛さ

かなわぬ恋の苦しみは
愛することをあきらめる悲しさ

愛する嬉びは　愛される嬉びより大きいはずなのに
誰もが愛されぬ辛さに　自分の愛まで失くしていく

それに気づかないあなたもまた
愛されない辛さに苦しいと涙する

与えられる愛は　決してあなたのものとなりはしないのに
与える愛だけが　あなたのものとなるはずなのに
あなたは　かなわぬ恋の苦しみに　愛することは無駄だと涙する

人が恋するのは　与える愛が欲しいから

恋することが　どれほど切なく悲しくても
あなたに今　恋する人がいて
あなたの愛が　あなたの胸いっぱいに拡(ひろ)がっていくなら
恋愛という言葉は　あなたのためのもの
あなたは　自分の恋を成就させている

あなたの恋が　愛で満たされていくこと
それは恋が実るということ
恋という小さな愛の種が　大きな愛の花を咲かすとき
人が恋する　その意味を知るでしょう
神から与えられた愛の尊さで
人を愛する嬉びで

愛より大切なもの　*YOUR SKY*

風のない部屋に
君の唄声が聴こえる
陽のない部屋で
君が微笑む

木陰にざわめく落ち葉のような
僕の心の迷いが　君の風に吹かれ　空を舞う

君の木洩れ日のような微笑みと
春風のような唄声が　僕の孤独を消し去っていく

君の優しさは　君の悲しみから生まれ
僕の悲しみは　君の優しさに溶けていく

君の唄声に
空が踊り　風となる
君の微笑みに
風が唄い　空となる

どこまでも拡がる君の空に　僕は包まれていく
僕の全ては　君の中に存在し
君は僕の中で　永遠の風となる

神は見つからずとも
神より大切なもの　それが君の存在なら
僕は神を必要としない

愛する事は　どこか遠い処に　置き忘れてしまった
恋する事など　もっと遥か遠くに………
なのに　君が居なければ　僕は存在する場所すらない

僕は君の空（そら）の中で
君の風に乗り　生きている

恋する事が　身勝手な愛なら
愛を求める時は　いつもが恋だと……

神が愛だというなら　僕はまだ孤独の中にいる

愛は　特別なものでなく
愛は　神のようなものでもなく
愛は　君自身を見つける手だてでしかない

神を求めるのは　愛を知らずに生きてきたから
愛を愛（いとお）しく思うのも　愛を知らずに生きてきたから

神が人に恋するなら
きっと君のように愛するだろう

君が僕に教えてくれた
木洩れ日のような笑顔と
風のような唄声が
僕に愛する事さえ忘れさせてくれた

君の微笑みに
空（そら）が歌い　風となる
君の唄声に
風が踊り　空（くう）となる

僕は君の空（そら）の中で生きている

儚き夢 *THE SUN AND MOON*

恋する者が　愛されることを願い
愛される者が　恋することを願う
けれど　人の恋は儚（はかな）くて
愛されぬ時　心失う

太陽が月を隠すように
愛は恋を消し去っていく
太陽のいない夜
愛に干渉されぬ夜
月は星と瞬いて　恋は自由な夢を見る

不毛なる我が心の大地に
幾つもの種子が降り注ぐ
愛なき心に　恋は実らず
恋なき心に　夢は届かず
夢なき心に　愛は育たず

ああ愛しき君よ
夢と夢の狭間で生き続ける君よ
太陽と月と星を背にして
水の中で燃えさかる炎を探している
振り向けば
太陽は宇宙を隠し
愛の前に　我が心を露呈さす

無数の傷に　心は結晶のように磨かれて
誰もの無意識まで映し出す

なのに
水晶のような月と
楽しげな星の光に彩られた
この宇宙は　神の如く美しい

愛を疑えば　恋を憎しみ
恋を抱けば　愛を疑う

決して昼と夜がひとつにならぬように
愛と恋も混ざり合わぬもの

それでも
夢は語りかけてくる

太陽と月と星が共に輝く空を
私の船が渡っていく
君の微笑みが流星の雫のように降り注ぎ
船の軌跡は美しい道となる

人の夢は儚くて
目覚めた時　君を失おうとも
人は夢を見続ける
神の夢にたどりつく　その日まで

CHAPTER 2

火の鳥の悲しみの章

THE SADNESS OF THE FIREBIRD

姿を変える不死鳥

あなたは風
姿を持たぬもの
あなたは風
姿を変えるもの
あなたは風
この世の果てまでも
あなたは風
あなたを抱きしめるまで

輪廻　*ANSWER*

愛し合って二人は結ばれた
男は女に優しく、女の心は幸せに満たされていた
時がたち、男の心から女への愛が薄らいでいた
女は気づかぬふりをしていたが、悲しい思いをしていた
やがて、男は別の女に恋をした
男は家に帰らず、女はひとりぼっちの夜を泣き明かした
ある雨の夜
男は不慮の事故に遭い、記憶の全てを失くした
女は男に別れを告げようとした
けれど、男は女の顔を見て微笑んだ
初めて出逢った時と同じ優しい目をしていた

男と女は再び愛し合った
以前と同じように、男は女に優しく、女の心は幸せに満たされていた
けれど、幾時が過ぎ、
男は再び恋人をつくり女の傍からいなくなった
ある雨の夜
女は病に倒れ、病室のベッドに横たわっていた
男は女の元に駆けつけた
女は男を見て微笑んだ
しかし再び、男が女の前に姿を現わす事はなかった

長い長い年月がたち、二人は再びめぐり逢い、愛し合った
女は男に優しく、男の心は嬉びでいっぱいだった
けれど、いつの頃からか、女の心は男から離れていた
女は寂しげな男の横顔に胸を痛めたが、
なぜ愛が冷めていくのか自分でも解らなかった
女は別の男に恋をした
女は家に帰らず、男はひとりぼっちの夜を泣き明かした
ある雨の夜
男は病に倒れ、病室のベッドに横たわっていた
しかし二度と、女が男の前に姿を現わす事はなかった

赤い糸　*VOICE*

ふたつの魂は肉体を得て人となり
ひとつは男に、もうひとつは女となった
そして、この地で出逢い、恋に落ちた
結ばれた二人は幾年の歳月を共に暮らし、
やがて心安らぐ場所に帰っていった

ふたつの魂は、再びこの地に舞い降りた
ひとつは女として、もうひとつは男として
なのに、なぜか二人は　すれ違いばかり
ふたつの魂が、この地で満たされることはなかった

二人は前世の過ちを繰り返さないため
今度は誰にも見えない赤い糸を結んだ
(彼ら自身にも見えないような……)
ふたつの魂は赤い糸を探し、様々な恋をした
しかし、赤い糸は見つからなかった
いや、赤い糸がなにかさえ、彼らには解らなくなっていた
この地に舞い降りて長い年月の経ったある夜、
二人は空を見上げ、つぶやいた
「なぜ人は生まれてきたのでしょう」
星の瞬きも　月の輝きもない静寂(しじま)の中に、二人の声だけがこだました
とても傍にいたのに、深い闇が互いの顔さえ見えなくしていた
けれど今、二人ははっきりと知ることができた
互いに約束し合い、探し求めていた相手なのだと

もしあなたが、今の恋に迷っているなら
目を閉じて　その人の声に耳を澄ましてみればいい
その声が、心地良くあなたの心の奥深くまで届くなら、
あなたの選択は　決して間違っていない
けれど、その声にしばしの安らぎさえ感じ得ないなら
あなたの選択は誤り
もともとあなた自身は、女でも男でもない魂の存在そのものだから
あなたが好きになるのも　その人の魂そのもの
容姿やかけひきに　惑わされてはいけない
赤い糸は魂の一部である心、その心を表現する言葉
そして、その言葉を伝える声の音色にあるのだから

君　*FOREVER II*

かつては　木の中に生まれた
深い森の中で光輝く妖精と呼ばれた君よ

かつては　岩の中に生まれた
気の遠くなるような寿命を全うした君よ

かつては　人の中に生まれた
嬉びと悲しみに心震わせたか弱き君よ

君よ
その魂の透明なるものよ
見る事も触れる事もできず
自分の心の欠片(かけら)さえ所持できぬものよ
女でもなく男でもなく
この地で
夢のように　その姿を変え続けるものよ

君は風の中にいた
君は花の中にいた
君は鳥の中にいた
そして今、君は人の中にいる

永遠なる生命の中で
幾度の生と死を繰り返し
君はいったい何処に辿りつこうというのか？

身を焦がすほど恋した事も
限りない愛しさに抱かれた事も
泣いた事も笑った事も
癒えることのなかった心の痛みも

死はまるで小石を捨てるように
いとも簡単に　君から全てを消し去ってしまう

ああ　何のため　君はこの地に生を受けたのだろう
僅かの歳月の中に　君はその答えを探し出せるだろうか？

全ての体験は死にかき消され
その記憶の欠片(かけら)さえ　君は失くしてしまうというのに
君のかけがえのない旅は　死が　無に帰してしまう
なのに　君は多くの旅を続けてきた

君の生命は　無意味なものなのか？
それとも　意味あるものなのか？

よく晴れたある朝
いつものように　君は花に水をやる

君がこの地で思いやる全てのものは　かつての君自身の姿なのだ

大地に寝そべり
満天の星空を見上げるとき

君が何を想おうと　その想いが君自身なのだ

君は美であり
君は愛であり
君は恋であり
君は孤独であり
君は悲しみであり
君は夢であり
君は星である

君は全てのものの中にいて
何ものにも束縛されない　空(くう)そのものなのだ

君は男でもなく女でもなく
獣でもなく　花でも木でもなく
君は透明なる空(くう)そのもの　陰りなき心の輝きそのもの
空(くう)である君は知っているはず

「得ること以上に大切なものがある」と

君のものになろうとも
君のものにならずとも
かけがえのないものが　この宇宙に存在していると、君は知っている

たとえそれが
君から　どんなに離れていようとも
そしてそれが
君に生命ある事すら知らなくとも
何ものにも勝る素晴らしいものが
この宇宙の何処かに　確固として存在していると、君は知っている

君がこの地で産声をあげたとき
何ひとつ不安を抱かなかったように
君は死を前にしても
何ひとつ怯える必要はないのだ

なぜなら

君は君から離れ　君へと戻っていくだけだから
君はいつも　君自身なのだから

死　*FUSION*

風の音に
耳を澄ませば
聞こえてくるでしょう　愛しき調べ

心　この星で
私という人となり　あなたという心を愛す
やがてこの躰(からだ)朽ち果てて　心　この躰に留まれず

あなたの目に　我が姿見えず
あなたの耳に　我が声聞こえず
あなたの手に　我が躰触れられず

心　この躰から去りゆけども
我が心　あなたの傍

躰　この地から去りゆけども
我が姿　あなたの傍

あなたの思い出の中に　あなたの瞼の中に　いつまでも

風の音に
耳を澄ませば
聞こえてくるでしょう　愛しき調べ

流れる雲　*EASY*

完全なるものよ
それは支配者として君臨するものなのか
それとも
我々と共に虚ろい続けるものなのか

形を変えない雲
朽ちない花
終わりのない生命
それが完全なるものなら
支配という言葉は　初めからこの世になかったはず

流れる風
枯れゆく花
死していく生命
あなたは誰からも支配されず　自由に生きている

ただ
だだっ子のように
無いものねだりをしているだけ
黒いものは白を欲しがり
白いものは黒を欲しがる

あなたを支配していたのは
あなた自身だったのだ

完全なるものよ
その美しさと生命の尊さは
あなたが自らの支配者であることを悟るとき

あなたの傍にある
言葉にできないほど　あなたの傍にある

なのに
悲しみが　嬉びが
あなたの心の中に生まれ
あなたを支配しはじめる
そして　あなたは完全なるものを欲しはじめる

あなたが天高く　神の名を呼ぶとき
自らの心の声が　あなたに届いているだろうか

あなたは自分以外に完全なるものを求め
より多くの幸へと導かれたいと思っている

永遠の生命を手にいれたとき
嬉びも消え失せると、
知っているはずなのに

形を変えない雲
朽ちない花
老いることのない生命

あなたが求める完全なるものは
凍りつくような時の中にあると、
あなたは知っているのだろうか

嬉びも悲しみも恐れも平安も
全ての心を　あなたが素直に受け入れるとき
あなたは何者からも支配されず
自分自身を支配することもない

完全なるものが
流れゆく雲のように
自由なるものであると気づくとき
あなたは心の中に　愛しいほどの安らぎを見つけるだろう

理由　*LIGHT*

花や木　鳥や獣
生きとし生けるもの
共に生きるため　死にゆくもの
君は言う
　人の生涯も変わらない　生きるために生きている
　それ以外何があるというのか？

遠い昔
遅い夜の始まり
入り江の月は白く輝き　星もまだ姿を見せぬ浜辺で
ふたりは出逢った
音のない風が心を揺らし　たがいの胸をふるわせた
一瞬に恋が生まれ　ふたりは愛し合いひとつになった

重なる胸の鼓動は神の息のごとく　宇宙の調べとなり
星は動き出し　夜空は輝いた

世界にまだ誰もいなかった頃
心を持つ者は　ふたりだけだった
ふたりを神と呼ぶ者さえいない時代（とき）
遠い宇宙の始まり
男と女は　失くした自らの片割れを探し求めて恋をする

恋する心が愛を育みはじめた頃
世界には　数えきれぬ程の男と女がいた

あなたが女性（おんな）として生を受けた嬉びと悲しみ
それは　あなたの片割れである私からもたらされるもの
あなたの最も愛する者　あなたの最も憎しむ者

誰よりも　あなたを知っているはずなのに
私は　あなたを泣かせてしまう
誰よりも　あなたを愛しているはずなのに
私は　あなたを傷つけてしまう

それでも
あなたが流す涙は　美しい星の雫となり
夜空を照らすその光は　人々の希望となるでしょう
そう言って　あなたの片割れの神は消えた

「共に生きるため　生まれてきた」
ふたりの言葉が　時間（とき）の風に散っていった

賢者である君は言う
　愛を学ぶため　人は生まれてきた

けれど　学ぶ必要のない愛もある
心を奪われるような何かに出逢えれば
そのときめきは　永遠に　この宇宙に輝き続ける星の光となる
やがて　愛が消えても　その一瞬は永遠なる宇宙（かみ）の調べとなる

神が人と呼ばれ久しい頃
男と女は意味もなく恋をした
儚（はかな）い恋は　生まれた理由さえ忘れさせてしまう

宇宙（かみ）の調べは誰にも届かず
日の立つ音さえ聞こえぬ世界で
人だけが彷徨（さまよ）ったこの時代（とき）に

再び　あの懐かしい風の匂いがした
音のない風が　ふたりの心を揺らし
静かな恋の予感は　心をふるわす風となる
男は女を抱きしめ　この一瞬が永遠であればと願った

愛が恋を消し去ってしまう前
夜空にひとつ　星のまたたきが生まれた

CHAPTER 3

神と預言者の章

GOD AND PROPHETS

空(くう)なる言葉を持つ者

言葉は裸身を覆う衣服のようなもの
我身を飾り　我身を守る
自我に覆われた言葉を捨て
素直な心をさらけ出せるなら
心は神の夢に輝き　神の言葉で満たされる

言葉　*ONE*

口で語る言葉は　君にさえ聴こえぬ独り言
心で語る言葉は　神に捧げる贈りもの

脳で覚えた言葉は　記憶にもならぬ君の影
心で覚えた言葉は　神と君のもの

自身の心に触れたいなら　心で見て心で聴くこと

心で見るなら　全てが見える
心で聴くなら　全てが聴ける

雨の呟きと　風の囁き
季節の微笑と　陽の合唱
星の歌声と　地平線の悲しみ

心で想うなら　全ては真実なのだ

君は「この世は不幸だ」と言った
神に君の声は聞こえない

君は「神などいない」と言った
神に君の声は聞こえない

心で語る嘘は　涙を誘う
口で語る嘘は　嫌悪を生む

「愛してる」
「愛してる」
言葉を文字にすれば　言葉だけが生き心は死ぬ

「愛してる」
「愛してる」
言葉を声にすれば　言葉だけが生き心は死ぬ

だから　心で見て心で聴かねばならない

神の前で嘘がつけないのは
鏡の中の自分の顔を　変えられないのと同じ

君は心に触れねばならない
君が自身の心に触れたとき　君は神とめぐり逢える

君は　その心で感じることができる
他者は自身で　自身は神だと

君は　その心で感じることができる
他者は神の似姿で　神の似姿は君自身だと

君は「人は理由（わけ）もなく愛することができる」と言った
神に君の声は聞こえない

君は「私の全てを神に捧げる」と言った
神に君の声は聞こえない

“神に捧げる”それは　神の最も嫌う言葉
なぜなら“神こそ君に捧げている”からだ
(君は他者で　他者は神自身)

“君を捧げる”対象は
神から見れば悪魔でしかない
(悪魔は決して　君とひとつになりはしない)

神に捧げるものは　君が心で覚えた言葉だけでいい
(君は神の中にいて　神は君の中にいる)

言葉はふたつの心をひとつにする

君が知り　神が知る
神が知り　君が知る

君は「神の心に触れたい」と言った
神も「君の心に触れたい」と言った

君が見て　神が見る
　　　　　神が見て　君が見る
神が聴き　君が聴く
　　　　　君が聞き　神が聞く
君が語り　神が語る
　　　　　神が語り　君が語る
神が語り　君が知る
　　　　　君が語り　神が知る

心で覚えた言葉は　君と神のもの
心で語る言葉は　神と君のもの

君が神に触れ　神が君に触れる
空気が混ざり合うように　光が融け合うように

まるで　神とくちづけを交わすように
君は神の心で想い　神は君の躰（からだ）で語るのだ

私　*ANOTHER ONE*

我が身を照らす　我が心

心の影　光に溶け　我とひとつになる
私の心　幾つもの光と影　織り混ざり
その正体さえ見失う

心を探せば
悲しみは　深まり
欲望は限りなく
孤独が愛を遠ざける

一点の煌(きら)めきさえ
朝露のごとく朧気(おぼろげ)な時間の中に身を隠す

私が誰であろうと　私は心そのもの
あなたが誰であろうと　私の心そのもの

あなたは私の心の中に　その真実を隠し
私は私の心の中に　自らの真実を見つけられず

この星と　月のように
太陽と　惑星のように
私は　もうひとりの私という衛星を持つ
つかず離れず　私は私のそばにいる

心　彷徨う私を見つめる　もうひとりの私
嬉びの中で　悲しみの中で　怒りの中で
我を忘れる時も
私は私のそばにいる
そして　静かに私を見ている

波のない海に身を浮かべ
波と戯れ　波に浚われ　波に沈む
私を見ている
同じ場所の　違う世界で　存在のない場所で
私の心は私を見ている

いつだったか
私は神を探していた
私自身の心さえ　見つけられぬ私が
我が心を知る神を求め　彷徨っていた

我を忘れるほど　恋に焦がれるように
私はいつも夢の中にいた

私の心は月の輝かぬ夜の闇の中で
無数の小さな星の灯りを拾い集めるように
何かに夢中になり
何かから逃げようとしていた

ただ　今と違う処へ
そう　いつも　今と違う処へ行きたかっただけ

私は私の心から　逃げようとしていたのだ

波は遥か遠くからやってくると信じていた
けれど　波は流れぬ水面のゆらめき
夢に見た　遥か沖は
波打たぬ　静かな凪が何処までも拡がっていた

海の終わる場所
足もとに打ち寄せる波の泡
そこは　唯一海の音が聞こえる場所

そして　いつも私がいた処
私の心は海に打たれる砂のように
音を立て　波に浚われていく
何度も、何度も、何度も、何度も…

ただ　私はいつも　今と違う処に行きたかっただけ

私の心を知るものは　誰もいなかったから
私自身でさえ…

我が心の姿さえ　見えぬ者が
我が心の声さえ　聞けぬ者が
どうして人の心を知ることができようか

我が心さえ　触れられぬ者が
どうして神の心に触れられようか

盲目の私は　何ひとつ真実を知らず
見知らぬものとの出逢いだけが
心　ふるわす嬉びだと信じていた
捨て去る事の哀れみさえ
繰り返す波のごとく　忘れ去っていた

今　神よ　あなたはここにいて
私を静かに見ている
今　神よ　あなたはここにいて
私の心の声を静かに聞いている

私の心を知った時
私は　私であり　私でなく　何ものでさえもなく
ただひとつの真実の心として　私を見ている

海原に拡がる　凪に月の輝きが射し
私の心を乗せた船の道標となる

満天下の溢れんばかりの星の瞬(またた)きは
かつて夢に描いた無数の煌(きら)めき
海に浮かぶ　星の灯りを
両手にすくい　見つめると
同じ星が　水面に輝いていた

私が望んだことは　幻のごとく
手のひらからこぼれ落ち
遠く彼方に　消え去っていく

けれど今
私が拾い集めた煌めきは
心の中で真実の輝きとなる
幻でさえ　その姿を真実の輝きにかえていく

真実とは　言葉でなく
真実とは　姿でなく
真実とは　我が心の帰れる場所

それは　私自身の心の光

我が心を知ったなら
我が心の真実を　我が心で見つめられるなら
神は　もうひとりのあなた自身

誰かを　神と崇める必要もなく
夢の中に　神を思い描く必要もない

あなたが　あなた自身の心の姿を
静かに見つめられるなら

あなたが　あなた自身の心の声に
静かに耳を傾けられるなら

もうひとりのあなた自身は神となる
足もとに打ち寄せる小さな波が
海そのものであるように

預言者　*ANYONE*

子供の頃、叔父と一緒にトランプゲームをした
最初は　叔父が手にした絵札の当てっこだった
叔父の大きな手の中に隠れたカードを
ダイヤのクイーンとかクラブのキングとか　見ないで当てる
……透視能力ゲームのようなもの
20回やれば20回とも言い当てた

そのうち叔父がトランプを手にする数秒前から
どのカードを選ぶのか解るようになった
……予知能力ゲーム

そして今度は、叔父が手にするだろう絵札を
順番に紙に書いてテーブルの上に置いた
もちろん　叔父には見えないように裏がえして
気味わるがりながらも　叔父は　10枚のカードを
順番にテーブルの上に並べてくれた
紙をひっくり返すと、私の書いた通りの絵札を
順番に叔父はテーブルの上に並べていた
私が無意識とも言えるほど思いつくままに書き連ねた絵札を、
叔父は順番通りに　神妙な顔をして選んでいたのだ
……それは単純な予知能力ゲームでもＥＳＰでもなかった

大人になって神の奇跡を感じる時、
私は　子供の頃遊んだトランプゲームを思い出す
そして　こう思う
もしかして　私も神の御心のまま生かされているのかもしれないと
自分の意志で、自分の心の赴くまま生きてきたと
神に対して断言できる者がいるだろうか

神の奇跡は　それを奇跡と解らせることなく、動かぬ風のように訪れる
まるで空のように　ごく自然に私の躰の中にある
私に貸しをつくることも、恩を売ることも、
私のプライドを傷つけることも、自尊心を失くさせることもない

人生のチャンスに出逢い　成功をおさめ、自画自賛に酔いしれるその時にも、
神は「よかっただろ」とか
「私のおかげだよ感謝しなさい」と、口にしたりしない

浅はかな決断に人生を誤り　途方に暮れ、失意の涙を浮かべるその時も、
神は「おまえのためなんだよ」とか
「心を取り戻すきっかけになるんだよ」と、口にしたりしない

神のすぐ傍に生きること
それは　神が見えないほど
神の気配さえ感じ取れないほど　自然に
人生の全てと共にあること

あなたの　嬉びも笑顔も
あなたの　悲しみも泣き顔も
あなたの　選択もチャンスも
あなたの　感情と思考も
そして　あなたの出逢いと別れの全ても
神の御心のままなのかもしれない

誕生の時、あなたは何の不安も抱かなかった
それは　あなたの魂が
すでに神と共に人生を歩むと知っていたから

死をも恐れる必要のないあなたは、
神の言葉を預かる者は
決して未来を予言などしないと気づくだろう
たとえ　それが災いであったとしても
「私の言葉は神の意志なのだ」と得意げにしゃべりはしない

神は　決して時を言葉に変えたりしないものだ
なぜなら、神は時を空(くう)に変え
私たちに　自由を与えてくれるから
時間を弄ぶことはできなくとも
私たちは　自由な空間を持っている
いや　空間の中で
私たちは　神を忘れるほど自由なのだ

けれど　決してあなたを忘れることのない神は
時間の中で　あなたに語りかけてくる
それが　神の語る未来なのだ

あなたが　神を発見したいなら
あなたの過去と現在を見つめてみればいい
どんな事実にも感謝の念を持ち　人生をとらえることができれば
あなたは　神を見出すだろう
そして理解する
あなたの人生に　無駄なことは何ひとつなかったと

いつの日か、神と共にあることに気づいたあなたは
言葉の大切さを知るだろう
それは同時に　神を愛する素直な心でもある

自らの言葉を　あなた自身が愛せるなら
あなたも　神を愛している
自らの言葉を　あなた自身が嫌うなら
あなたは　神を愛してはいない
神を信じようともしない

あなたは　自らの言葉をあなたの心で聴くことで
神の声を　聴いている
あなたは　自らの感情と思考を聴こえぬ心の言葉にすることで
神の声を　聴いている

あなたは　いつもいつも神と共にある
そんなあなたは　いつの日か
誰もが神の預言者であると知るだろう

師　*GOD*

神との出逢いは、たとえそれが
夢の中のほんの数秒にも満たない出来事でも
残された人生の時間の中で、最も印象的な体験として　記憶に刻まれる
その声さえ耳にしたことのない神の姿を、
私は夢の中とはいえ　はっきりと見ることができた
——私が夢を見たのでなく、神が私に夢を見せてくれた
そんな特別な感動を　私は覚えた
年輪を連ねる樹木の葉が　その枝を隠していくように、
歳を重ねていくにつれ
夢の中で見た神の姿は、そのイメージを複雑なものとした
しかし　不思議なのは
神を思い出そうとするたびに、私の心は　純粋さを取りもどしていたことだ
神を思い描くたび、私の心は　全てを忘れ　素直になれた
遠い昔、夢で見た神は　良心とか道徳とか愛とか、そんな言葉では
とても語りつくせはしない　強いなにかを教えてくれた
それはかつて　誰も想像さえしたことのない、神の真実なのかもしれない

あるうららかな春の日
私はひとりの老人に出逢った
私が会釈をしようとしたずっとずっとずっと前から、私を知っていたかのように
彼女は私の名を呼んだ
彼女の声は　とても懐かしく、私の心の奥深くまで届いた
彼女が私の名前をすでに知っていたことへの驚きさえ忘れ、
私は子供のように微笑んでいた
まるで　小さな冒険の旅から帰った子供が　母親の前ではにかむように

それ以来、私は彼女のもとに何度も足を運んだ
彼女の言葉は　いつも同じだった
「素直な子よ、感謝と思いやりを忘れずに」
いつしか、私にとって彼女は　夢の中で見た神そのものとなっていた

そんなある日
奇跡は　何の前ぶれもなくやってきた
私は　神の姿を再び目にしたのだ
今度は夢でなく　現実の中で、神は　私の視界いっぱいに、その姿を現わした
なにも語らず、ただ私を見つめていた
もの言わぬ神の目は　私が無の存在であることを教えてくれた
神の視線の中で、時間は止まり　空間は静止した

永遠の時間を創造する　無限の空間
無限の空間を創造する　永遠の時間

永遠は無であり　無は永遠であり続ける
神は永遠と同時に　無の存在でもあった

神を傍にして　私は宇宙を知った
それは悟りでもなければ真理でもなく、ただ神自身の姿なのだった
私にとって　神は永遠と無のごとく、
触れるには大きすぎる存在となった

何度目かの夏の午後
私は風鈴の音を聞きながら　黙って彼女の前に座っていた
目の前の彼女も　まぎれもなく　神の姿そのものだった

神は永遠であり一瞬
神は無限であり一部

心は一瞬であれど　永遠に届き
躰は一部なれど　無限に拡大していく

生命は産まれ　永遠となり
生命は死して　無限へと溶けていく

私の生まれるずっとずっとずっと前から、神は私の傍にいつづけたのに
私は　神の存在を感じることができなかった。
この目で直接　自分の顔を見ることができないように、
神は　私と一体でありつづけたからだ
神は　私の目であり、私の顔は　神の姿そのものだったのだ

誰もが　鏡の中でしか自分の顔を見ることができない
しかし、誰もが自分の目に映る神の姿を見ることができる
ただ大切なのは、神に感謝し
全てのものを思いやる心に包まれているかどうか
その想いは人を無にし
無は無限と永遠に届き
宇宙全てへと拡大していく

無があるからこそ　永遠なる時間は続き
無があるからこそ　無限なる空間は拡がっていく

無我とは、感謝と思いやりに　我を拡大すること
無我とは、我を　宇宙と同化させること
無我とは、我を　永遠かつ無限なる神とひとつにすること

永遠なる時間の中で
無限なる空間の中で
果てしなく拡がる神の姿を　我がものと感じられるその日まで
無は存在し続ける

無が０でなく
無が無限であり
永遠である神の姿そのものであることに
気づくまで

悟り　*BIRTH*

夜に目覚め　深い悲しみと
過ぎ去った時間を　共有する者よ
日の立つ音に　目を閉じ耳をふさぐ者よ

まだ　触れられぬ期待に胸ふるわせ
真理の声を探し求める者よ
渇望は強い飢餓となり　まやかしさえ信じようとする者よ

幸せは　悟りは　迷いなきあなたの心にある
迷いこそ　苦しみ悲しみそのものなのだから

悲しみを消したければ
悟りを開きたければ
迷いを消せ
迷いなき人こそ　幸多き人であり
悟り人と呼べるものだから

月が地球が太陽が
そして　限りなき数の惑星とすい星が

果てしない時と
果てしない空に
その軌跡を持つように

無限の宇宙の中で
無数の星々が
寸分の迷いもなく　時空のリズムを刻み続ける

それが　自然すなわち神であり
その自然の摂理こそ　悟りそのものなのだ

だから

恋するなら　迷いなき心で恋せよ
愛するなら　迷いなき心で愛せよ

迷いなく恋する事で　苦しみは消え
迷いなく愛する事で　ひとつの悟りが開けていく

こうしてあなたは
幾通りもの悟りの道を歩んでいく

陽が降り注ぐように
風が雲を消すように

決して　死の淵にあっても
迷いの心なきように

宇宙がそうであるように
自然の摂理がそうであるように

あなたの心に　迷いの欠片(かけら)ひとつなく
あなたの動きに　迷いの影ひとつなきように

あなたが悲しみから　遠い処にいられますように
あなたが迷いから　とてもとても遠い処にいられますように

子供の頃
想い描いた見果てぬ宇宙は
あなたの心そのもの

心に浮かぶ想いの
ひとつひとつが
輝く星でありますように

あなたの心と身の動き
そのひとつひとつが
自然の摂理と共にありますように

悟りとは　迷いなき心と躰(からだ)そのものなのだから

かつて
あなたにもひとつの悟りを開いた時がある

誕生の時
発したあなたの産声は
何ひとつ迷うことなき　生命の悟りそのものだった

あなたは　迷いなき心と身で
この地に生命を宿したのだ
なにひとつ迷うことなく　幸多い人生を歩むように

CHAPTER 4

光と闇の始まりの章

THE BEGINNING OF LIGHT AND DAKRKNESS

なぜ天使は悪魔となったのか？

光を映し出す者よ
暗黒の夜空に浮かぶ
黄金の月のように
純粋に　その姿を
我が目にさらし出す者よ

光を映し出さぬ者が
暗黒の夜空のように
その心が空(くう)でしかない切なさを
あなたは知っているだろうか

神の部屋　*WHITE CANVAS*

死にゆく者よ
やがて影を捨て去る者よ
あなたは光に融け　無から無限へと旅する天使となる

死にゆく者よ
やがて影を失くす者よ
あなたは闇に混ざり　永遠の苦痛を知る悪魔となる

肉体が影を持つように　肉欲は闇を生む

影を持つのは　あなたが生きている証し
闇を持つのも　あなたが生きている証し

悪魔であるあなたも　初めは天使として生を受けた

自らの心に自由な絵を描いたあなたは
その生命と同時に　嬉びと悲しみをも描いてしまった

この世で再び天使となるのも悪魔となるのも　あなた次第

無地のキャンバスを額に入れ飾る事
それを無意味な事だと思うなら　神の部屋を訪れてみるがいい
そこは白紙のキャンバスが　辺り一面に飾られているところ

神の部屋で　あなたが青い空を描こうと
緑の大地を描こうと　影を生む事に変わりはしない

遠い昔　天地創造はこうして行われた
無地のキャンバスは　この世で唯一影を持たぬもの
それは純粋な神の領域で神自身の姿

影を持たぬ神は　決して姿を持たぬもの

あなたが自らの影を捨て去った後も
あなたの前に　白いキャンバスは現われ続ける
そして
あなたが再び絵筆をとる時
計り知れない神の愛の尊さに
自由というかけがえのない神の愛に
あなたは感謝できるだろうか

優しさ　*COOL*

あなたの優しさは
あなたの知っている限りの冷たさの裏返しである事に
あなたは気づこうとしない

あなたの冷たさは
あなたの知っている限りの優しさの裏返しである事に
あなたは気づこうとしない

あなたの優しさが
あなたの知っている限りの冷たさの裏返しであると
悪魔は知っている

あなたの冷たさが
あなたの知っている限りの優しさの裏返しであると
天使は知っている

あなたが優しき人になればなるほど
あなたは冷酷な手管を理解する

あなたが冷酷な人になればなるほど
あなたは優しさの手立てを理解する

優しさをひとつ学び　冷たさをひとつ知る
冷たさをひとつ知り　優しさをひとつ学ぶ

陽の輝きが暗い影をつくるように
あなたは優しさから悪魔の姿を見る

暗い影が陽の輝きから生まれるように
あなたは冷たさから天使の姿を見る

優しき人よ
あなたの中にも　悪魔は棲み
冷たき人よ
あなたの中にも　天使は宿る

あなたの心は
まるで神そのものであるかのように
天使も悪魔も同時に受け入れてしまう
そして
あなたという心の中で
天使も悪魔も　あなたというひとりの人となる

影　*WORDS*

光に我が身を照らし出すように
光に我が心を映し出すものよ
目を閉じるほど目映い光は
深い影を君の足元につくり
心はその闇に溺れ
君は再び光を求めるだろう
どれほど強い光も　君の影を消し去る事はできず
ただ深い闇をつくり出すばかり

君が光である事を願うなら
闇の苦しさを知らねばならない

優しさは足元に映る影の如く　君と共にある

君が嬉びなら
影は君の苦しみ

君が天使なら
悪魔は君の影

目を閉じた時　何が見える
耳をふさいだ時　何が聞こえる
口をつむった時　何が語れる
君の心の内側に
光が届かぬ深海のような心の奥底に
差し込む光の姿を　君は見るだろうか
差し込む光の音を　君は聞くだろうか
差し込む光の真実を　君は語れるだろうか

君の心の中から生まれる
光の姿が　光の音が
君自身である事に気づく時
君は闇の中からも　光が生まれ出る事を知るだろう

光とは輝きでなく　光とは言葉であり
神の心そのものなのだ

君の躰(からだ)は神の心であり
君の心は神の言葉であり
光も影も　神の心の場所に存在する
神の躰自身なのだから

光　*UNIVERSE*

宇宙が誕生する前
永遠なる光だけがあった
その色に区別はなく
その輝きに強弱はなく
光は何処までも均一に果てしなく拡がっていた

ある時
ひとつの光の粒が弾けるように輝き始めた
それは驚くほどの早さで　その色を濃くし　その輝きを強めていった

いつしか
ひと粒の光は強烈な輝きを持って　あたり一面を燦然（さんぜん）と照らしていた
光が光をもって　光を照らし始めたのだ
近くの光は　我知らず輝きを増し
遠くの光は　我知らず闇となった
光が光を持って　光と闇を創り始めたのだ

気がつけば
それが永遠の終焉
すなわち宇宙の始まりだった
そしてそれは　光と闇の始まり
嬉びと悲しみ　愛と憎しみ
善と悪　生と死　神と悪魔の始まりでもあった

宇宙が無から生じたものなら
無とは　永遠なる調和であって完全なる神の姿

宇宙が時空を刻み込むものなら
時空とは　調和の破壊であり永遠の破滅

時間が動き始めたのも
空間が膨らみ始めたのも

永遠なる調和が崩れ去ったから
それは完全なる神の崩壊

宇宙の始まる前　闇はなく光だけだった
なのに
光が自らの手で闇を生んだのだ
たったひとつの強烈な光の粒が
穏やかに輝いていた光を　闇の存在へと変えていったのだ

偉大なる光＝偉大なる神　の出現は深い闇を呼んだのだ

完全なる神よ
あなたは何故に
永遠なる調和を捨て去り　この世界を創り出したのか

闇を消し去るため　光が必要なら
神よ　あなたはその輝きを増やせばいい
しかし　目映い光は深い闇を生むばかり

その答えに気づくまで
あなたはただ輝き続けるばかりなのか

朝　眠りから目を覚ますと
穏やかな陽の光があった
目を閉じると光は消え　私は再び闇に包まれた
闇の中で　私は陽の輝きを探した
すると　瞼の奥すみに
光の残像がキラキラと輝き始めた
それは柔らかな輝きだった
闇の中で　優しい光が風のように心地良かった
私はその輝きを見失わぬよう
目を閉じたまま　その光を見つめ続けた

再び瞼を開けた時
陽は沈み　辺りは夜の闇に覆われていた
けれど　私には見えた
暗闇の中で　穏やかに灯り続けている光の輝きを

闇の中の光の姿が
いや　いつしか闇と呼ばれるようになった光の姿が　はっきりと見えたのだ

光の中に闇はなく
闇の中に闇はなく
あるのは穏やかな光だけ
光を遮るもの　それは自我という盲目の心

私は知っている　光も闇も心の中にある事を

完全なる神よ
あなたは光の中にもいて闇の中にもいた

完全なる神よ
あなたは永遠の光の中から　かけがえのないものを生み育てた
それは　あなたがくれた最高のもの
自由とは　神がくれた私達の自己宇宙
私の心は宇宙そのもの　それはあなたの愛そのもの

愛する驚き　愛する嬉び　愛する苦しみ　愛する勇気
愛する悲しみ　愛する正義　愛する過ち　愛する幸せ

あなたは今も　愛という永遠なる調和となり
全てのものの中で　穏やかに輝き続けている

光の中で闇の中で　私達はあなたと共にある

宇宙の終焉に闇はなく
あるのは光だけ
闇とは輝きのない光の姿
闇の中に輝く光が見えるなら
今すぐにも　宇宙は
永遠なる調和の中で　息づいている事に気づくだろう

愛　*WORDS II*

遥か昔
宇宙の終焉と始まり
愛の粒子は光となり　光の断層は時空となった

時間と空間は表裏のごとく　宇宙という存在の場となった
時空は神の言葉の舞台であり　言葉達は姿を得た

神の言葉に初めて影が生まれ　言葉は自我となり　自由気儘に振る舞った

言葉と言葉が惹かれあい　言葉と言葉が傷つけあい
欲望の淵で享楽と失楽が混在した
愛を失なくしたものは愛を怖れ　愛を捨てたものは愛を疑った
愛を掴み愛を失くし　ただ元に戻っただけなのに
世界は空虚なものとなり　存在の価値さえ無いという

神は静寂の中に鎮座し　言葉達から身を隠した
神が目を伏せると宇宙は暗黒に覆われ　全ての輝きは消え失せた

主を失くした言葉達は神を探した
我が身が神の言葉のひとつであることを知らず　神を追い求めた
時に愛するものの中に安らぎを見つけ　その中に神を見出した気がしたが
愛の真実を見失ったものに　神を見つけることは出来なかった

愛より幸せなものも　愛より辛いものもない
言葉達は神を求めるように　愛を求め愛を呪った

神の涙は再び言葉となり　暗黒の宇宙を彷徨う星となった
神の鼓動は時空を揺るがし　宇宙は動き始めた

星は衝突し　言葉は砕け散り　神の涙は銀河となり
宇宙を色のない光で照らした
神の言葉の多くがこの世界から消えていった

言葉達が愛したのは自分自身だった　愛さなかったのも自分自身だった
世界は無数の言葉で溢れていると思っていた
それは言葉の真実を知らなかったから

神がひとつの言葉であるように　この時空に言葉はひとつだけだった
自らの奥深い処に存在し　感情と思考の源であり
引力のように自我をつなぎ止めるもの
愛は言葉となり　姿となり　万物となった

今　神の涙は雲となり　私の頭上にある
私は鳥となって　天高く空に舞い上がる
雲のかけらを掴み　口の中に放り込む
希望と安らぎに満ちた味がする

風の歌声が聴こえる
雲は流れ星は微笑み月は踊り愛は溢れ　言葉は無数に生まれ
真理は雨の如く降り注ぐ
銀河は美しく輝き　宇宙を彩り始めた

CHAPTER 5

永遠の終結と始まりの章

THE END AND BEGINNING OF ETERNITY

無から生まれ
　無に帰れる
　　幸せ

愛から生まれ
　愛に帰れる
　　喜び

この生命は
　永遠に輝く
　　星の光となる

宇宙創造　*FIRST LOVE*

初めに愛があった
空間も時間も何もない無の中に　愛だけがあった

あなたが生まれる前
誰にも見えぬ処に
愛が満ちていた
あなたの父と母の心の中に

あなたの生命がこの世に誕生する前
父と母の愛があったように
宇宙誕生の前に
神の愛があったのだ

あなたの生命が
宇宙という生命に生まれたひとつの花の種なら
あなたも宇宙そのもの
空間と時間は　あなたと共にある

空間は
宇宙という生命の躰(からだ)そのもの
時間は
宇宙という生命の鼓動そのもの

あなたが成長するように
空間は膨張していく
あなたが脈打つように
時間は刻まれていく

空(くう)の中でまどろみ
時(とき)の中で眠りにつく
あなたが生きていくこと
あなたが死んでいくこと
この時空の中の永遠のひとつ

全てが存在する前　愛だけがあった
愛の中から生まれたあなたは　愛の中に帰っていくだけ

やがていつの日か
宇宙も眠りにつく
そして帰ってくる　あなたのいる場所に

あなたと宇宙は　再びひとつとなる
空間も時間も光も音もない無の中で

静かな愛の調べを聞きながら

宇宙の死　*NEW UNIVERSE*

生命に

生と死があるように
宇宙にも生と死がある

生命の死は

その躰を構成する細胞が
ゼロになるのではなく
死が訪れた時に
その細胞は腐敗し分解していく

そして分解した物質は
別の生命体へと取り込まれていく

宇宙の死はどのようなものだろう

現在　宇宙は

膨張していると考えられている
今後　果てしなく膨張を続けていくのか
ある時　縮小へ向かうのか
すでに縮小を始めているのか

しかし宇宙の死は

この世の全てのものに死があるように
必ずやってくるもの

宇宙の死
それは　この時空の死を意味する

生物は

小さなひとつの授精卵から細胞分裂を繰り返し
成長し　死を迎えるが
授精卵のサイズまで縮小する事はない

時空の死も

この宇宙が始まった時の大きさまで
縮小する事なく訪れるなら

ある日突然

この宇宙の時間と空間が静止する時
それが宇宙の死と言えよう

生物も物質も
それが存在する時間と場所を失ってしまう

すなわち
全ての死がやってくるのである

「凍りついた時空」

それが宇宙の死とするなら
凍りついた時空は
やがてボロボロと崩れ落ちていく

その後に何が残るのだろう

神は

ひとつの細胞が分裂して　６０兆の細胞になるように
神は　ひとりの人間が成長し神になる夢を託して

ひとりひとりの人間に自由な意思を与え
さらなる神を創造しようとしているのかもしれない

無限に拡がる神なる宇宙を創造するために

神の消える時　*NAME*

『物質は波動が凝縮したものである』　（20 C量子力学）
『初めに言葉ありき』　（新約聖書）

自然界に存在する万物全てがその名を持つのは
神の言葉により創造された証し
言葉は心からこぼれ落ち“存在”となる
万物は神の言葉が具現化した神の心の絵姿なのだ

そして　私達人類は
この自然界の知り得る全てのものに名を付けてきた
なぜ神は　私達にそれを許したのだろう
その答こそ
私達がこの宇宙に生まれてきた理由を　知る手がかりとなるに違いない

昔も今も
私達は花や鳥　星や銀河にまでその名を付けてきた
また、この自然界に現われる様々な現象にも名を付けてきた
そして　知ってか知らずか　私達はそれを自然の法則と呼んでいる

神の法則は　神の心を持つ私達の心の中にも存在しているのだ

私達人類が　万物にその名を付けることができるのは　神の心を持つ証し
私達の心は　風や海や花や木や鳥や獣と同じだけ　神と近い処にある
そして　この宇宙の調和の中で　万物がそうであるように
人類には　私達だけにしかできない　大切な役割を担わされているのだ

私達のこの耳は　自然の声を聴くためにある
私達のこの口は　自然の言葉を語るためにある

私達はその意味を知らなければならない
なぜなら　人類は
永遠なる神の心の語り部であるからだ

いつかいつの日か
この宇宙も終焉を迎える日が来るだろう
それは　神の消える時
しかしそれは　新たなる宇宙創造の始まり

かつて　神の声を聴き
神の言葉を語り
そして
神の心を決して忘れようとしなかった　誰かの心に
再び言葉が生まれ　さらなる幾つもの宇宙の始まりとなる日

万物は“その人”の心に生まれ　言葉を得て“存在”となるのだ

いつしか
私達は“その人”に名を付けてこう呼ぶだろう
“神”と

けれど　私達が
何処から来て　何処に行こうとしているのか
その答を知るには　再び長い長い時間を必要とするだろう

しかし　私達には忘れてはならない事がある

私達がその人を神と名付け得たその理由を
決して忘れてはならないのだ

自由　*THE CREATION*

陽を浴び輝く緑
本能に身をまかせ飛び交う鳥
沈みゆく太陽と瞬き始める星々

今　私の視野に映る全てのものは　自然と一体化している
なのに　人間である私は自然とひとつになれず
ある時は自然に逆らい　ある時は自然に怯え　生きている

私は“私が何者であるのか？”思いを馳せる
神の躰(からだ)であり自然のひとつである“私”が誰なのか考えている

たぶんそれは　私の指先にある豆粒ほどの小さなホクロが、
「私は誰？」と問いかける姿に似ているだろう
「おまえは私のホクロだよ」
神は私にきっとそう答えるだろう
けれど、ホクロである私は言う
「私はホクロであって、あなたでない」と
「私は人間であって、神ではない」と

神は自然であって　自然とは存在する全てのもの
すなわち　私自身も神の躰の一部なのだ
それは　わかっているつもり

イエスは言った
“汝の隣人を愛せよ”

自分と他の者を分けへだてなく愛する事で　自己は拡大する
私は隣人を愛した
かつてホクロだった私は　指先一本くらいまで愛を拡大した

そこで私は問う
「私は誰？」

「おまえは私の指先だよ」
神が答える

「私は指先であって神ではない
　私が神だというなら神の姿を見せてほしい」

神は鏡を差し出し　こう言った
「私を見たければ自分を見ればよい　ここに私が映っている」

鏡に映っているのは、小さな指先だけだった

「それが私なのだよ」
神は言った

「私は指の先っぽであって、決してあなたではない
　あなたが私に知恵を与えなければ、
　私は悩む事なく　花や木や鳥や獣たちと同じように
　あなたという自然と一体になれたのに
　なぜあなたは私にこのような思考を与えたのですか？」

「おまえは今、ただの指先だと言ったね
だけど私には、単なる指先であるおまえが考えるなんて、到底思えない
今おまえが考えているという事は、私が考えているという事なのだ
おまえはただの指先かもしれないが、おまえの心は私の心でもあるのだ」

「それでは、あなたの脳を見せてください」

「脳を見せても、おまえはそれが神の姿とは思わないだろう」

「どうすればいいのですか？
まさか『この宇宙全てを自分と分け隔てなく愛せよ』とでも言うのですか
この僅かな寿命の中で、それはとても不可能な事ではありませんか」

「感謝の想いは、時には愛の力に勝る時がある
おまえが、ただ生きている事に感謝する事、
それは自然界全てを愛するより　価値ある事かもしれないからだ」

「感謝が愛より価値のある事なのですか？」

「私は今、こうして息をしている
考えてそうしているわけではない
私の心臓は脈打っている
それも、私が考えてしているわけではない
私が歩くのも、左足今度は右足と考えて歩を進めているのではない
それは全て、私の自然なる行為なのだ
おまえにも神経はあるだろう
おまえ達が生きるための自然な行為をつかさどるものが
私の意識は眠ることなく、絶えずこの躰、いや自然全てのものに注がれている
空も雲も大地も花や木も鳥も獣も、そしておまえ達人間も全て私自身であり、
私の意識そのものなのだ」

「そうかもしれません
もしあなたが私に知恵を与えなければ、
花のように無条件で　あなたと同化できるでしょう
しかし、このように神の存在を疑う事も、
そして人を傷つけ、時には殺し合う事もあなたの意識だというのなら、
どうしてあなたに感謝などできるでしょうか」

「おまえが私を疑う事も、おまえ達が傷つけ合い殺し合う事も、
全て自分が自分を疑い、自らを傷つけ合い殺し合う事となるのだ
おまえ達が疑おうが信じようが、おまえ達が殺し合おうが仲良くしようが、
こうしておまえ達は私と一緒にいる
私といる限り、おまえ達に真実の死はない
細胞は死んでも　生まれてくる
殺し合っても　新たなる細胞は私と共にある
私にとって、おまえは　新陳代謝を繰り返す私の細胞そのものなのだ
おまえが細胞のひとつだと思うなら、おまえは再び生まれてくる
本当の死とは　私が死ぬその時だけなのだから」

「あなたが死ぬまで　私の輪廻転生は終わる事がないというのですか」

「おまえが細胞のひとつに名前をつけるなら、輪廻は巡るだろう
しかし、おまえが自分を神である私だと思うなら、輪廻を繰り返す事はない
もっと分かりやすく言うなら、おまえが自分自身を私だと思えるかどうかだ」

「しかし、それに迷い悩む事も　あなたの思考なのでしょう」

「けれど、おまえが信じる事も　私の思考なのだ」

「なぜ、そんなまわりくどい事をするのですか
花や木や鳥にそんな試練はないのに
私達人間も　そんなふうに創ればよかったではないですか
そうすれば、自然界はあなたという神の平和な世界に成り得たはずなのに」

「おまえは自由を考えてみた事があるか
自由とは、全てを受け入れ愛する事だ
そして自由とは、全てを投げ出し愛する事だ
自由とは、選別しながら生きる事ではない
私は自由そのものなのだ
時間と空間、生と死、私は全てを生み出し、全てを失くす
それが私なのだ」

「この世に起こる不幸・災難　そのどれもが
あなたの自由な意志によって起こるとしたら、
それは神の気まぐれとしか思えません
気まぐれな自由が神なら、私は神を信じない」

「おまえがそう思うのも自由だ
そして、それも私の意志のひとつなのだ
ひとつだけ言っておく
自由を消し去れば、私の存在する意味もない
おまえがもし、幸せを夢みなければ苦しみは生まれない
しかし、嬉びとの出逢いもない
神も必要としないはずだ
全てが最初から平和で平安であり続けるなら、
誰も神の必要など考えようともしないだろう
神がこの自然がすなわち宇宙が永遠に続くものなら、
初めから何もなかったのと同じなのだ
死のない処に　神は存在しないのだ」

「宇宙が終焉を迎える時、あなたも死ぬというのですか？」

「そうだ
宇宙こそ私自身なのだから
そして生も死も私自身なのだから」

「その時、万物の輪廻も終わるのですね
輪廻転生を繰り返す不死鳥の生命も終わってしまうのですね」

「おまえの輪廻は続くだろう」

「ええ！　宇宙万物の生命は神と一体であると言ったあなたが死ぬ時、
私の生き残る場所はないはずではありませんか」

「おまえを残し、全てのものは　私と共に消滅してしまうだろう
花や木や鳥や獣も、そして無数の星たちも
しかし、真実を知ったおまえは存在するだろう」

「どういう事なのですか？
時空のない処に宿る生命など、想像もできないではないですか
それとも　私が時空になるとでも言うのですか」

「おまえには自然界を見続ける目があり、
自然界の音を聴き続ける耳があり、
英知を養い　記憶を持つ脳がある
そして、言葉を語る事のできる心がある
やがて　私の心を理解するおまえは、私と同じ宇宙と成り得るだろう
そして　私のように、自らの中に自由な世界を創造し、
自由とは自らの宇宙である事に気づくのだ」

「私の心から片時も離れないこの苦悩は、
その為にあなたが与えたものなのですか」

「おまえたち人間は、私という宇宙に生まれた花の種なのだ
おまえはやがて　私という神からの束縛を受ける必要もないほど、
真実の自由を得る事ができるのだ
おまえはただ　心の中に、おまえが望む自由な夢を描けばいい
私がそうしたように……」

子供の頃からいつも　考えあぐね悩んでいた事がある

「私は何処から来て、何処へいくのか？」

その想いは大人になった今も変わらない
かつて、私の問いに答えてくれた神がいた
彼は、自分は宇宙であり　自然であると言った

やがて、彼の言ったとおり、彼は去っていった
神は消え、宇宙も消滅した
時空もない世界に、私ひとりだけが残った

「私は何者であるのか？
私は何処から来て、何処へ行けばいいのだろう？」

今、その答えが私の傍に浮かんでいる
いや　その答えこそ、私自身そのものなのだろう
私は自分に言い聞かせるように言った

「私は自由なのだ
何も恐れる事はない」

初めに言葉があった
次に自由が創造され、宇宙が生まれた

私の宇宙　*ANOTHER LOVE*

この場所の　この時間(とき)の中で
あなたに逢う事はできず
始まりと終わりと永遠があった
あの場所の　あの時間の中にあなたはいた

けれど　あの場所もあの時間も
私に与えられた　あなたの一部

あなたは生の中に　死の中に
　　　　光の中に　闇の中に身を隠していた

あなたの誕生は　あの宇宙の始まり
あなたの死は　あの宇宙の終わり

私の場所も私の時間も
あなたの一部であったはずなのに
今　あなたはいない

恋は愛の始まりにもなれば
恋は愛の終わりにもなる
恋と愛は　月と日のように
心の全てを照らし続けた

恋とは　競い合う自我のようなもの
求めるものは全てが恋だった
愛とは　ひとつになろうとする自我のようなもの
失ったもの全てが愛だった

闇は光の始まりにもなれば
闇は光の終わりにもなる
光と闇が重なり合うように
愛は姿を変え　あなたはいつも私のそばにいた

私の希望の中に
　　絶望の中にあなたはいた

私の嬉びの中に
　　悲しみの中にあなたはいた

私の友の中に
　　敵の中にあなたはいた

私の親の中に
　　子供の中にあなたはいた

石の中に　水の中に　花の中に　風の中に
笑顔の中に　涙の中に　夢の中に
思うもの　見えるもの　聴こえるもの　触れるもの
全ての中にあなたはいた

あなたは　求めてやまぬ夢のようだった
あなたは　決して手にする事のできぬ夢のようだった

誕生の時　始めて目にしたのは　あなただった
死にゆく時　最後に触れたのも　あなただった

遠い昔　いや　この瞬間なのか
私には思い出せない
それは　私があなたを必要としなくなった時間
それは　あなたがあなた自身を必要としなくなった場所

光は闇に別れを告げ
愛は恋に別れを告げた

あなたの誕生は　あの愛の始まり
あなたの死は　あの愛の終わり

愛が愛に別れを告げた時間
私が私自身を必要としなくなった場所

嬉びと悲しみがひとつになり
慈しみと憎しみがひとつになり
生と死がひとつになり
無と無限がひとつになる

君に想像できるだろうか
新しい宇宙の始まりと　新しい愛の始まりを

未来と過去と現在がひとつになり
光と闇がひとつになり
恋と愛がひとつになった　時空の存在を

今　あなたのいない　この場所のこの時間の中で
私はひとりたたずみ

私は誰なのか
私は私の姿を思い描いてみる
消えゆく記憶の彼方に
ふと　あなたのあの懐かしい香りがした

私はありのままの私を想像しよう
あなたがあの時空を創造したように

空なる本　*SYNCHRONICITY*

あなたがいたこの部屋で
あなたの好きだった百合の匂いがした
けれど目に映るのは　閉ざされた空間と静止したような時間の影だけだった

あなたは時間という道を歩み　生命というページを綴る
生涯をかけ　一冊の本を書き上げる

死を前にして　あなたの心は自らの人生を自由に行き来し
再度　あなたという一冊の本と巡り逢う

たとえそれがどんなものであれ
そして　それがあなたと共に消えゆく儚いものであれ
この上もなくかけがえのないものである事をあなたは知る

あなたという空なる一冊の本

あなたの人生が　空であるがゆえにあなたの心は無限である
あなたの心が　あなたの人生において真実そのものであったように
神の心は　この宇宙において真実そのものであり続ける

この宇宙の一つであるあなたは　神と心を共有し時空を共にする

空は重なり　時間となり
時は連なり　空間となる

宇宙の真理を理解出来ぬあなたにも　心の意味は全て理解出来るはず

愛と嬉び　怒りと悲しみ　美と欲望………
あなたは誰からも学ぶ事なく知っている

あなたが誕生する前からあなたは知っている
あなたがその躰を持つ前から　あなたは心と言葉を持っていた

心に浮かぶ言葉の全ては　神の姿であり宇宙の真理そのもの
あなたの空なる一冊の本は　あなたの心の姿でありあなたの真実そのもの

心は見えぬ時のように　時間と共にあり
躰は透き通った空のように　空間と共にある

あなたの心は時の如く　あなたの躰は空の如く　神と共にある

躰は心を得　生命となり
空間は時間を得　時空となる

時のように神と心を共にするあなたは　空のように神と躰を共にする

あなたの目の前に拡がる世界は
あなたという心が織り成す　あなたの言葉の全てなのだ

宇宙と共時性　*SOUL GRAVITATION*

この宇宙さえ存在なき処に神の心あり
心は言葉となり
言葉は形となる

始まりは愛で　愛は光となり
光は時間と空間になる

その行く先は宇宙の膨張となり
愛は無限なる宇宙の拡がりとなる

神の心は自然と呼び名をかえ万物の姿となる

神の愛は万物の魂となり生命となった
神はその愛を形にかえ宇宙すべての存在となったのだ

ゆえに存在すべてが愛なのだ

万物が神の愛の姿なら
万物の持つ引力とは神の愛そのもの

あなたが神の愛に触れるということは
あなたの魂が少しでも神の心に重なるということ

その瞬間
あなたの言葉は形を持ち
あなたの言葉はストーリーを生む

なぜならあなたの魂も神の愛の結晶
神がそうであるように　あなたの言葉も存在となるからだ

それは眼にしたこともない輝き

その輝きを覆いつくす肉体とその欲望
光さえ星の引力に引き込まれるように　愛さえ肉欲に歪められてしまう

神の愛から生まれた肉体が神の愛を覆いつくす
けれど　その肉体さえも神の言葉で創られたもの

愛から生まれた肉体に感謝なき者に神への感謝もない

愛を知る為　愛を失い
幸を知る為　幸を失う

愛されることを知っても　愛されぬことを知らず
幸せの中にいて　不幸を知らず

それらはすべて愛からほど遠い

愛から遠い場所　それは闇
闇は悲しみや苦しみの中にあるのではなく
慈悲なき心の中にあるのだ

眩く美しい輝きだけを光だと思うなら　あなたは闇の人
清く正しい心だけを愛だと思うなら　あなたは闇の人

自然(かみ)はそれを教えてくれる

あなたの魂に神の心を映すには　あなたの愛が傷負うしかない
ダイアモンドを研磨するように　あなたの愛に無数の傷を付けるしかないのだ

あなたが神の愛を知るなら
あなたの言葉は存在となる

神の愛は引力を持ち
言葉を呼び寄せ
言葉は存在となる

EPILOGUE

難解なるものの儚くも美しい真理の章

THE FLEETING YET BEAUTIFUL TRUTH OF ABSTRUSENESS

光と影が交差し
時は刻まれ
存在の全ては記憶となり
時空の内側へと置き去られていく

未来はまだ訪れぬ存在の影
まだ輝かぬ月の影

私の記憶に届かぬ未来は
私と同じ時空に存在する
まだ輝かぬ昼の月

心帰れる場所　*UTOPIA*

何の為　生まれて来たのか？
幼い頃　何度も自問した
その答えを見つけられぬまま　君は歳を重ね
誰もと同じように　ただ苦しみを避け喜びだけを探し続けた

限り無き欲望に支配される自らの奴隷のように
君の心は決して安らぐ事がない

ゴールを知らぬランナーのように
変わらぬ円盤の上を回り続ける時計の針のように　君はひたすら走り続ける

いつしか君は人生を競争のように捉え
人に勝ることを喜びとし　人に劣ることを不幸とした

君の幸せは君ひとりでは成り立たず　常に比べる相手を必要とした
君の幸せも不幸も君の内になく君の外にあった

底の抜けたカップに注がれる水のように　君の感情は心を素通りしていく
心を育めぬ君は盲目の旅人のように　人生をさすらう
死の足音が聞こえた時
ゴールの見えない君に死は限りない不安となる

君は再び人生の意味を考える

人生は死の前にゴールを探す旅である
人生の終着点は死ではなく　心帰れる場所にある

君が大切なものを失くしても
心をそこにおけば　何も失っていないことが解るだろう

君が闇に覆われても
心をそこにおけば　闇など存在しないことが解るだろう

誰もがそこにたどり着くため　この世に生まれ躰を持った
肉体に付帯する感情のすべては　心がそれを見つけるためにある

ある吹雪の朝
舞い上がる雪の中にひとりの老婆を見た

「こんなに寒く視界もきかぬ雪の中
あなたはいったい何処に行こうとしているのですか」
「行こうとしているのではなく　帰ろうとしているのです」

暖かなその声は迷い子は私だといった

帰れる道を持つ者に　人生は幸せな旅となる
行く道しか持たぬ者に　人生は果てしなき彷徨いとなる

心帰れる場所を持つ者に　死は安らかな眠りとなり
心帰れる場所を持たぬ者に　死は受け入れがたき恐怖となる

ずっとずっと昔から　私の魂は心の中に帰るべき場所を探し求めていた
心はそれに気づかず　何処か遠いところにある幸せを掴もうとしていた

感情が何処に移ろうと　全ては心に帰ってくるように
君がいくつ輪廻し姿を変えようと
魂の帰る場所は今の君の心にしかないのだから

自由な心　*SANCTUARY*

どこまでも見渡せる大地に立ち　偽りの衣を脱ぎ捨て
吹き抜ける風と陽の温もりを肌にし　我が心唄う

自由と束縛の間を行き来し
笑顔と泣き顔を同時に持った彷徨い人よ

今　お前はやっと帰るべき家を見つけた

春の砂塵に目を閉じるように　現実に目を伏せていたお前は
今　春の歌う風と草木の口笛を耳にし　心躍らせる

灼熱の陽の眩さを嫌い　陰の中に身を隠したお前は
今　冬の雪に覆われた静寂と影の無い世界に　心震わせる

遠い昔　愛する君が私の心の傷になったあの時から
私は　幻の海を渡り　蜃気楼の港に船を着けてきた
幻想と現実の狭間を泳ぎ　理想は儚い夢でしかないと思っていた

いく人もの出逢いと別れがあり　いくつもの笑いと涙があった
優しい人に逢い　冷たい人に逢った
賢い人に逢い　愚かな人に逢った
嘘をつき嘘をつかれ　真実を話し真実を聞いた

だけど　私の手は誰よりも冷たく
誰かの心に触れるたび　さらに冷たくなっていった
それは私が私自身に嘘を付いていたから

大切なものを嫌い　どうでもいいものを愛そうとした
未来を見ながら過去を思い　優しさに触れながら自分のことだけ考えていた
ある嵐の過ぎ去った夜　蒼い闇の中で若かりし君と逢った
涙がとめどなくこぼれ　喜びと愛しさだけが心に溢れた

晴れ渡る秋空は青に塗られた白　海の輝きと霧を映し出す
吐息かすかに白く　風冷たく　幸せの予感に心弾ませる

この空を抱き締めるように　君を抱ければどんなに幸せだろう
この空にくちづけるように　君にくちづけ出来ればどんなに幸せだろう

今　私は西に向かうこの道に立ち　暮れなずむ空の美しさに心奪われる
朱色の虹は淡く空を染め木々は影絵となり　やがて全てが夜に溶けていく

この道の行きつく先は　夜の闇の中
この心の行きつく処は　死の静寂の中
いや　この道の行く先は　黄昏のように心美しい君のいる場所
この道は　私の心の奥深くつづく　私だけが知っている私だけの道

貴方は完全なるこの宇宙を創り　不完全なる心を宿したと思っていた
だけど今　理解する
不完全なるものこそ貴方の夢
自由にならぬものこそ唯一の神の自由であることを

風の音がする　陽の匂いがする　貴方の声が聞こえる

「誰にも従わぬ者よ　いや従えぬ者よ
お前のその夢と絶望こそ私のまだ見ぬ世界
お前は私に創造されながら誰のものでもない
欲望にも良心にも支配されぬ者よ　お前はその自由をどこから得た？」

我知らず駆け出していく　この道のまっすぐ彼方に
この道を帰り　私は君に逢いに行く
この道を辿り　もういちど君に逢いに行く

心があなたを傷つける　その心はあなた自身
心があなたを狂喜さす　その心はあなた自身

心は肉体に隠れ　あなたを自由にあしらう
自由にならぬ心を　自由にならぬ自分自身を　あなたは魂と呼ぶ

あなたは苦しみを誰かのせいにする
しかし　あなたを苦しめるのはいつもあなたの心でしかない
あなたは喜びを誰かのおかげだと言う
しかし　喜びをもたらすのも常にあなたの心でしかない

あなたは心を肉体から生まれ肉体と共にあるもの、と思っている
しかし　心は肉体から生まれたものでも　肉体に付随しているものでもない

الجمال　Красота　Schönheit　美しさ　Làm đẹp　Ομορφιά　아름다움　יופי
زیبایی　Kagandahan　Uzuri　Գեղեցկություն　Beauty

حزن　Печаль　안타까움　Tristezza　Θλίψη　עצבות　غمگینی　Lungkot　Huzuni
悲情　Nỗi buồn　切なさ　Տխրություն　Tristețe　Sadness

أمل　Надежда　희망　Hoffnung Espoir　Ελπίδα　תקווה　امید　Pag-asa　Matumaini
希望　Esperança　Hope

その呼び名を知らなくても　その意味をあなたは知っている
美しさと醜さを　あなたは教えられることなく見分けられるように
切なさの意味も希望の意味も　あなたは最初から知っている

なぜなら　あなたの心はあなたが生を受ける前から存在し
あなたはその心に触れるだけ　だから

心は天地が創造されるずっと前から存在していたのだ

この宇宙の生まれる前　いくつもの心が生み落とされた
全ての心が形を持たぬまま　永遠のような時が過ぎた

いつしか神は心に姿を与えた
初めに無の中で愛が一点の光となり　光の影は闇となった

無数の喜びと悲しみが　一点の無の中から爆発するように溢れ出た
音が生まれ時間（とき）が誕生し　静寂が現れ　空（くう）間が生まれた
それは　宇宙が誕生し　生と死が生まれた瞬間

やがて　無数の心は万物に姿をかえ　生命を持った
無数の心は言葉に隠れ　生命の種となった

神の心に全ての言葉が存在するように　この世界には神の全てがある
無と無限　生と死　光と闇　過去と未来　始まりと終焉　愛と憎しみ
相反する言葉がひとつの心から生まれ
星のごとく無限の方向に飛び散っていく

真理は幻のごとく答えを変え　宇宙は夢のような謎に満ちている
あなたが神に触れたと思ったとたん　神はあなたに姿を変える
神を探す術をなくしたあなたは　偶像の神を祀りあげるしかない

あなたの自由にならぬ魂　自由にならぬ自分自身は　神の心そのものなのだ
誰もが自由に出来ないもの　それが神であり　あなた自身の心そのものなのだ

あなたの求めてやまぬ神は　あなたでしかないのだ

あなたはその心を　神のものとすればいい
あなたの喜びを　あなたの悲しみを　あなたの優しさを　あなたの涙を
あなたの全てを　神のものとすればいい
あなたが神を思う時　あなたは万物の中に有る

あなたは自由そのもの　あなたは神がみる夢の中の神そのものなのだ

鳥になり空を舞い　風になり季節を旅し　流星になり宇宙を駆け巡り
そして　愛しき人の心の中でそっと眠りにつく

道　*MY HEART*

夜空に星が生まれるように　この世界にあなたの道が生まれる
原野を進み大地に道ができるように
人生の時間を歩みあなたの道が生まれる

海に海路があり　空には空路がある
しかし　あなたはいつもその足で歩き続ける
時には立ち尽くし絶望の淵にいる
時には飛ぶように駆け抜け有頂天でいる

あなたがこの世に生まれた時　あなたは道の始まりに立った
あなたがこの世から消える時　あなたはこの道の終わりに立つ

始まりと終わり　この道にはあなただけがいた

私はいつもこの道の遠くを見ていた
私の前にある現実（いま）を見ないで
あなたの肩越しに見えるこの道の遥か彼方を見ていた

私の前に光が射し　私の後ろに影が出来る
希望は未来にしかなく　ここにあるのは夢の欠片だけだと思っていた
一歩一歩の幸せに気付こうとせず　明日を追い求めてばかりいた

いつも自分を許し　人を許さずにいた
私の心は私を見ず　常に人の心を見ていた
疑いは私を通り越し　いつまでも人の心の中にあった

美しさは欲望の種で　神が創造したもの
醜さは絶望で　人の心が生みだしたもの

美しい君よ
偽りの言葉で飾られた心は腐っていないか
臭わない悪臭と　見えない汚れをどこで払うのか

心ない言葉で語りかけると　空虚な言葉が返ってくる
真実の心で語りかけるなら　真実の心が返ってくる

真実の言葉で自分の心に語りかけるなら　何が返ってくるだろう
良心とは神の一部なのか
それとも私の勝手な思い込みなのか

私の良心は　全てのものの良心に置き換えられるだろうか
私の神は　全てのものの神と成り得るだろうか

あなたの心にいる私に問いかける
けれどそれは 真実の私でなく私の良心でもなかった

愛する人よ
心の真実を分かち合い　共にこの道を歩けたらなんと幸せなことだろう

なのに　私の道を歩む者は私しかいない
私がどれだけあなたを愛そうと
私があなたの人生を歩むことが出来ないように

美しい風に姿はなく
香る春の草に　散りゆく秋の葉に　そよぐあなたの黒髪にその姿をたくす

目にする美しさと　決して目に出来ぬ美しさ
優しき心と強き心　全てのものの中にその姿をたくす

銀杏の葉が風に舞う
冬はもうそこまで来ている

木漏れ日が　まるで神のくちづけのように暖かい
私は目を閉じ　あなたの優しさを抱き締める

光は道の彼方にあるのではなく　私のすぐ傍にある

甘い幻想　*ISOLATION*

幼き頃
君の想いを心に描けば
風は清く　空は高く　陽は輝いた
生命は希望に満ち　人生は何処までも続く真っ直ぐな道のようだった

なのに　今　君の心は終わりのない旅をする

夢を得る者は
夢を失くし

夢に届かぬ者は
夢を得る

求めたものへの君の愛と情熱が　夢と共に消えていく
夢はあたりまえの世界となり　君は人知れず新しい船を出す

浜辺に立ち　大海原の彼方を夢見る
満ちゆく波が君の足元を濡らすと　君は無造作に手で拭う

君の夢が自ら　君の身体に触れたというのに
君にはその思いもなく　喜びもない

君が拭ったそのしずくが　夢見る大海原の一部であることに
君は気付こうとしない

希望は　君の心の内側にあるべきはずなのに
いつも君は　心の遠くに夢を見る

終わりなく繰り返す幻想の中に　君の安息の日々はない
終焉のない人生は永遠の彷徨い

死だけが君の人生を終わりある旅にする

喧騒なる世界に放たれた心を　やがて時間（とき）は静寂の彼方に誘っていく

無に帰すため生きて来たのか
君が人生で思い描いた夢は　今　何処にある

薄れゆく意識の中で
消え去った過去の断片が懐かしく　まるで宝石のように輝き出す
それはやがて涙の粒となり　君の心を洗いつくす

掛け替えのないものを置き去りにしてきた君は　誰かの夢となり得ただろうか
愛された優しさや愛しさが込み上げてきて　君はひとり泣きつくす

君は最後の夢を見る
君が求め　君を愛してくれた人たちのあの幸せな笑顔とめぐり逢うために

君の求め続けた平安は　今　君の心の内側にある
ずっと孤独だった君の　あの平凡で懐かしい想い出の時間の中に

夢のごとく *THE DISAPPEARING PENINSULAR*

晴れた秋の日
彼女は水中に根を張る草木の中に彼を案内した
彼は水の上に建てられた木の歩道を歩き
遠くからの景色との違いに驚き　ここには人の居場所が無いことを悟った
夏でも寒い日が多いこの場所に　花が咲くのはほんの僅かの間
冬になればすべてが白く覆われる

遠い記憶の中で　彼女は水の草原に立つ彼を見たと言う
彼は小さくはにかんで　彼女の澄み切った瞳に魂の過去を託す
水面が陽の光を反射して万華鏡のように輝いた

野鳥が鳴き　オジロワシが矢のように飛び立つと　すぐに日が暮れていく
彼は冷たくなった手をこすり帰り支度をする
夜の帳はもうそこまできている
彼は暖かな部屋と温かい食事を思い　彼女の手を取った
彼の手は冷たかったが彼女には暖かく感じた
時間は光のごとく早く過ぎ去り　心を過去に置き忘れさせてしまう

年老いた誰もが口にする　人生は長くて短いもの
時は過ぎ去り
いくつもの過去は時間の川に漂う小舟のように記憶の中で揺らめく
死に背を向ける者は　置き去りになった船に乗る

過去に心を奪われた者は　影を持たぬ亡霊のように欲望の淵を彷徨う
かつて　愛は眩いばかりの光の中にあった
今　愛は閉ざされた闇の中にある

人は限られた出逢いの中で人生の意味を摘（つ）むんでいく
出会いは全てが突然なるもの
しかしそれは必然なる運命のめぐり合わせ
出会いの数と　出会いの順序だけの物語がある

風が水面を揺らし波立つように
あなたは運命にいくつかの驚きを与えようとする
生きているということは　あなたを想い慕うこと

永遠なる時の流れの中で生きるということ　それはほんの一瞬の時
誰にも語られる事のないひとしずくの雨粒のようなもの
まるで無と無限の狭間で揺らめく幻のように
心は儚い夢のごとく消え去っていく

夏の嵐の夜
彼らは海辺の部屋にいた
彼女は傷つき二人の間には目に見えない壁があった
沈黙を切り裂くように　白い稲妻が夜空に走った
雷鳴轟く中　彼女は怯えた顔で青く輝く海を美しいと言った
彼が窓を開けると　湿った風が吹き込み彼女の頬を濡らした
彼は彼女を抱きしめ　永遠のような時間を感じた

愛しき君よ　その心は誰のもの

やがて消えゆくこの半島に海鳥が舞う
遥かなる人よ
かつてここに人が住み
いくつかの喜びと悲しみがあった事をあなたは知るだろうか

湿原に沈みゆく太陽と　昇りゆく月
西の空を染める美しき夕映えと　瞬く星
ここは夜と昼が重なり　光と闇の交わる場所

北から吹く風に微睡むと　何処からかあなたの声が聴こえてくる
冷たい空に口づけると
神の吐息が風となり
私の心は舞い踊る木の葉のように神の言葉を奏ではじめる

マルチバース　*SYNCHRONICITY II*

私たちの信じる自然科学は　人間の五感を通じて得られる情報を
人間の脳で分析し結論付けたもの　それが万人の常識となり真理となる

もし鳥や獣が世界観を持つなら　彼らの真理は全く違ったものとなる
人間の五感を遙かに超える感覚を持つものにとって
この世界はどのように映るのだろうか
人間より遙かに高い知能を持つものにとって
この世界はどのように考えられるのだろうか
彼らから視て私たちの英知は
私たちが獣を見るごとき稚拙なものに見えはしないだろうか

私たちの知る真理は　人間にとっての真理でしかない

もし一生で一度起きるか起きないかという偶然が
ある日を境に頻繁に起き続けるなら
もしあなたの想像する世界が目の前に広がっていくなら
あなたはこの世界の偶然を偶然と捉える事が出来るだろうか

たとえばあなたが何気なく古いアルバムを開きふと初恋の人を懐かしむ
その数分後玄関のドアを叩く音が聞こえるとそこには初恋の相手が立っていた
彼は昨夜あなたの夢をみて数十年ぶりに訪ねて来たと言う

たとえばあなたが旅に出る
そこで偶然ある良き人に出会い満たされたひと時を過ごす
数か月後あなたは再び旅に出る
そこで偶然別の良き人と出会い幸せなひと時を過ごす
その次の旅でも、その次の次の旅でも、、、
幼い頃母親を脳の病で亡くしたあなたは精神に問題を抱え
友人のひとりも持てなかった
今あなたは旅をするたび充実した愛しい時間を取り戻していく

だけどあなたが出会った人々にはあなたの知らない共通点があった
それは誰もがあなたと会った後　時を待たずして亡くなっていたことだ
彼らはみんな余命幾ばくかの脳のガンに侵されていた

良く晴れた午後
公園で本を読んでいたあなたは空を舞うシャボン玉を眼にする
30分後読書を終えたあなたの目線の先には
さっきと同じシャボン玉が空に静止するかのように浮かんでいた
あなたがシャボン玉を凝視すると
シャボン玉は夕闇に見えなくなるまで飛び続けた
翌日図書館で床に落ちていた本を手に取ると
あのシャボン玉そっくりな絵があった
それにはヒエロニムス・ボスの描く天地創造三日目の地球と書かれていた

その日からいくつもの共時性が起きる度
あなたはあの割れないシャボン玉を思い出す

晴天の空にシャボン玉を見つける事は出来るが
夜の闇の中に見ることは出来ない
シャボン玉は自ら輝くのではなく　光を映し出すだけだから
あなたの心が空のように透明でその想いが穢れなきものなら
あなたの想いは誰しもが目にする存在となる
あなたの心が闇に満ちその想いも闇深きものなら
あなたの想いを目にする者はいない

闇の中で自らの姿さえ眼にする事が出来ないあなたは
意識だけがあなたを証明する手だてでしかないことを知る
あなたの心から闇を払えば心は光に溢れ　透明な想いは光を映し出す
シャボン玉が陽の光に輝きその姿を現すように
あなたの想いも神の光に映し出され姿形となる
あなたの想いは神の愛に照らされ存在となるのだ

シャボン玉が光を映し姿を現すように　あなたも神の愛によって姿となった
この世の全てのものは神の愛の中にある
なぜなら目に映るものは全て神の光を映し出しているから

それでもあなたは　この世界の全てのものは時空の中にあると考える
時間は過去から未来に向かうもので空間は時間の重なりだと　あなたは考える

しかし時間も空間も存在を映し出す鏡のようなもの
あなたが自由に未来にも過去にも想いを馳せる事が出来るように
あなたが宇宙の果てまで想いを馳せる事が出来るように

全ての存在するものには　過去も未来もなく無も有もないのだ
全てのものは時空という鏡に映る意識の姿
鏡が光なき場所では鏡となり得えないように
時空も神の愛なき処で時空とならず

この一瞬の瞬きのような輝きの中に　全ての時空が存在する
時空の向こうには
無と呼べるほど透明な神の心に浮かぶ　無限なる神の想いがあるのだ

The Kiss of God

PROLOGUE

Dreaming and Drowsing

夢とまどろみの章

Random scribbles

When dreaming

Quietly looking back

At the smiles of one's childhood

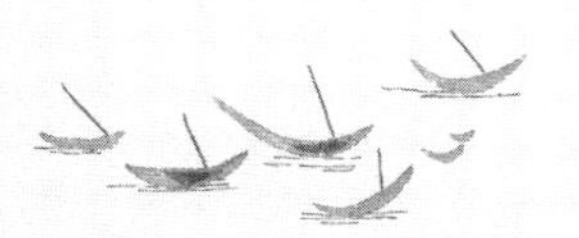

To Dream *PROOF*

I say it is easy to dream
You say people who can dream are fortunate

If you can dream
Even in sorrow
Before long
Sorrow will leave you
But
What can you do
When you even forget to dream
And cannot take a step forward from where you are?

The sun rises Winds blow Clouds drift Time passes

Among the twinkling stars
Even quietude begins to shine beautifully

Nature speaks to you even when you are in tears

Telling you it is easy to dream
To simply look at things as they are with your pure heart

Nature's melody like God's sigh
Embraces you softly and gently

You are breathing
Cradled by the breath of the vast and boundless universe

The fact that you are sad
Proves
You are alive
And that
One day you'will remember you were right beside God

If you can dream with your pure heart bedewed with tears of sorrow

When I was young
I turned my eyes
Only to the world outside

I never thought seriously
About my father
Or my mother

I was never affectionate
To the people near me
Nor to the things I had come by

My heart was always full of curiosity
And seeking
For fresh surprises

Becoming
makes things far
and becoming far-
nearby difficult to
are out of balance
just by slightly
point of view
"Eyes are
to the

As I grow older
I have begun to turn my eyes
Only to the world around me

I think so seriously
About my son
And daughter

I no longer
Earnestly try to make
My dreams and desires come true

My heart hates to be disturbed at all times
And I have begun to reject
Changes from outside

near-sighted
away look blurred
sighted makes things
see because your desires
Your vision will return
changing your heart's
After all they say
the windows
soul"

The radiance
of the full moon without a single cloud
People see the perfection of the beautiful divine
moon and call it an exquisite moon But the full moon's
strong radiance erases that of the Milky Way and of other
constellations On some nights, the half moon seems beautiful
On some nights, the crescent moon seems beautiful On some
nights, the countless stars twinkling in the pitch-dark sky of the
new moon seems beautiful One night, when you have no anxiety
about the glory of your long and yet short life, you shine like the
full moon and forget your tender heart One night, when you
encounter your love, your love's happiness will become your
happiness Your love's sorrow will become your sorrow
Your heart will have another heart like the half moon
Soon on the night your dearest child is born
your heart will be willing to sacrifice
yourself for your child

Like the
crescent moon
your heart becomes
the foundation to support
your family And on the
night you leave this world
you will come to know that
there are numberless stars
twinkling in the night sky
Your heart exists without a
form like the new moon
You just watch the world
quietly till God's light
shines upon you
once again

Deep Blue *TIME FOR ME*

The end of night
The beginning of morning

On such
Transient moments

With no shimmering moon
With no shining sun

The horizon disappearing
The sea and sky turning into one deep blue

The universe in a drowse
Quiet sigh

A time just for me
I think of you

After separation
The end of joy and sorrow

As though left behind
Even from time

Tears forgotten
Smiles forgotten

The memories of one's life disappearing
The past and future turning into one deep blue

Love in a drowse
Quiet sound of the breeze

A time just for me
I think of you

A Beautiful Star *FOREVER*

Snow began to fall at the end of night
Enclosing sorrow within cold hours
Teardrops turned into little dews of solid ice
Another teardrop fell beyond the night sky and disappeared

It took me a long time to come and see
The place where the wind started to blow
And where the wind stood still
Deep in your eyes, sad but yet calm, I saw profound compassion

During the hours that had started to go by
I stayed away from you whenever I was sad
I kept you away from me whenever I felt joy
But now
Just as I can hear the sound of the stars twinkling
I can hear your heart beating
Just as I can see the wind dancing
I can see your heart shining

Your compassion was born from your sorrow
Your tears turned into stars scattered in the night sky
You know
Where the stars are born
And where the stars disappear

When your tears filled the night sky
Compassion brimmed over
And the light of the starry sky like sunshine
Bid farewell to the long night

Your sorrow is because of the place where the wind stays still
Your joy is now with the wind that is about to blow
Your warm teardrops have melted the frozen snow
Time hovers in the sky as it touches the wind and you are beside me smiling

There is a sense of pathos even in love
Knowing that parting will come to pass
The time we spent together will disappear like the stars at sunrise

Just as death follows every life
Sadness is felt in every love
But I will never forget
The fleeting time within eternity that I spent with you
Your compassion changes even static time into wind and it has taught me
"Soulful love makes everything heartfelt and turn them into pure love"

My loved one
The joy of having encountered you
Will become a beautiful star shining forever in the eternal night sky

CHAPTER 1

The Sadness of Love's Shadow

愛の影の悲しみの章

Why do people fall in love?

Affection is dedicated to others
Romance is dedicated to oneself
In our limited time
Within eternity
We are longing for
The joy of meeting our loved ones

A Rose by the Window *MYSELF*

There was a man in love
As the roses growing in the field were so beautiful
He picked one rose and offered it to the woman he loved
She smiled
"What a beautiful rose!"
From that day on, he picked a rose every time he went to see her
After a few days, she stopped expressing her joy with words
Still the man could not forget her smile and kept on giving her roses
One day
He found a bunch of roses withered away like waste in the corner of her room
He decided to ask her why
Although it took him lots of courage
"Don't you like roses any more?"
"............"
She did not answer him
Maybe not because she could not answer him but because she did not want to
He left her room and silently closed the door
When he saw wild roses swaying in the wind on his way back
He felt that he had lost something but had also found something important

There was a woman in love

As the roses growing in the field were so beautiful

She picked one rose and decorated it by her window

The man pulled her into his arms without noticing the rose by the window

Still she continued to decorate her room with a rose whenever he came to see her

But after a while, roses had simply disappeared from her room

The man had stopped visiting her

She asked herself why

Although it took her lots of courage

"Doesn't he like me anymore?"

"............"

She did not give any answer to her own question

Maybe not because she could not find an answer but because she did not want to

She sat by the window and gazed out into the field

Roses were no longer blooming anywhere

She had even forgotten that the season had changed

She felt she had lost something but had also found something important

Her Other Self *LOVE MYSELF*

When she fell in love
'Her other self' was within her
When he fell in love
'His other self' was within him

In order to love 'her other self'
She had loved 'his other self'

But she had not realised this

Her love was directed to herself
For which she needed to be in love

She had fallen in love with him in order to love herself

Being in love was important for her
But for him her love was not true love

She wept when he left her
Yet she never thought about where her tears came from

In her heart, she could only feel the pain of loneliness

She had merely returned to herself
When 'her other self' within her had disappeared

This she had not realised
She was simply in so much despair for having lost him

She was sharing her joy
Not with him but with 'her other self'

She was sharing her agony
Not with him but with 'his other self'

She was talking not to him but to herself

So she bound him with jealousy and blamed him for all her discontent
Not doubting that she was actually giving him pain in order to love herself

For her, succeeding in romance meant controlling him as she desired
The aim of her romance was to make him her shadow

For not being able to love herself, she bound herself to a spell named 'romance'
And it became a tool to make someone else love her

The word 'self-love' belongs to her, who cannot love herself

Loving someone out of fear of not being able to love oneself will not bring true love
Yet romance is still one kind of love

The Kiss of God *THE REASON OF FALLING IN LOVE*

A woman in love unknowingly
May see the illusion of God in the man she loves
Opening her whole heart and giving him her whole body
Sometimes nestling up to him, crying in front of him or turning for his help

Telling him what she cannot tell anyone else
Showing him what she cannot show anyone else
She becomes an honest woman in front of the man she loves

As if she were offering herself to God
Her body and heart is dedicated to the man she loves

A man in love unknowingly
May see the illusion of God in the woman he loves
Opening his whole heart and loving her with his whole body
Sometimes nestling up to her, showing fear in front of her or turning for her help

Telling her what he cannot tell others
Showing her what he cannot show others
He becomes a truthful man in front of the woman he loves

As if he were offering himself to God
His body and heart is dedicated to the woman he loves

Because they cannot encounter God
Because they want to take possession of God
Men and women fall in love

The yearning for God they are yet to meet creates love in people's hearts

For the woman he loves
For the man she loves
Everyone becomes a semblance of God at least once
But
They return to be ordinary people

In the man she loves
In the woman he loves
Everyone sees the love of God at least once
Still
They realize that they are just ordinary people

Women falling in love many times
Men falling in love many times
Those seeking for God and those sought after as God

How wonderful it would be
To become the illusion of God at least during a kiss
Like God yearned for in the state of nothingness and forever

Romance *FLOWER OF LOVE*

The distress of not being loved
Is the distress of not being able to love

The pain of unrequited love
Is the sadness of giving up love

To love should bring more joy than to be loved
Yet people lose their feeling of love due to the distress of not being loved

Having not realised this
You also shed tears of pain due to the distress of not being loved

Love given to you will never become yours
Only the love you give will become yours
Yet the pain of unrequited love makes you weep as you think love is vain

People fall in love because they want to give love

No matter how heartrending and sad it is to be in love
If you are now in love
And your heart is full of love
The word 'romance' is for you
You have fulfilled your romance

When your romance is filled with love
Your romance will blossom out
When your little seed of romance blooms into a big flower of love
You will understand why people fall in love
For the preciousness of love God has given us
For the joy of loving someone

YOUR SKY

In a room where there is no wind
I can hear you singing
In a room where there is no sunlight
I can see you smiling

Like fallen leaves rustling in the shades of trees
My wandering soul is swept by your wind and swirls about in the sky

Your smile like sunbeams shining through the trees
And your voice singing like the spring breeze wipes away my loneliness

Your kindness was born from your sadness
My sadness melts into your kindness

To your song
The sky dances and turns into the wind
To your smile
The wind sings and turns into the air

Your boundless sky embraces me
My entire self exists within you
You become the timeless wind within me

Even if God is not found
If your presence is more precious than God
Then I do not need God

I have left behind my affection somewhere faraway
As for romance, somewhere even further away...
And yet if you are not here I will not even have a place to exist

I live in your sky
Riding on your wind

If romance is a selfish kind of love
Seeking for love would always be a romance ...

If you say God is love, I am still in solitude

Love is nothing special
Love is not something like God
Love is only a way to discover yourself

People seek for God because they have lived without knowing love
People long for love because they have lived without knowing love

If God were to fall in love with a person
God would probably love the way you would

You are the one who has taught me
Your smile like sunbeams shining through the trees
And your voice singing like the wind
Have made me forget even affection

To your smile
The sky sings and turns into a wind
To your song
The wind dances and turns into the void

I live within your sky

A person who is in love wishes to be loved
A person who is loved wishes to be in love
However, people's romantic feelings are transient
They lose heart when they are not loved

Like the sun hiding the moon
Affection effaces romantic feelings
A night without the sun
A night not affected by affection
The moon and stars twinkle, romance dreams as it pleases

On the barren land in my heart
Several seeds fall
Romantic feelings do not blossom in a heart without affection
Dreams do not reach a heart without romantic feelings
Affection cannot be fostered in a heart without a dream

Oh, my loved one
You who continue to live in between dreams
With the sun, the moon and the stars in the background
You are looking for a blazing flame in the water
When you turn around
The sun has hidden the universe
Revealing my heart before love

The heart is polished like a crystal with innumerable scratches
Insomuch as to reflect everyone's unconsciousness

Even so
The crystal-like moon
And the universe colored with joyous starlight
Have god-like beauty

To doubt affection is to hate romantic feelings
To have romantic feelings is to doubt affection

Like the day and night never crossing
Affection and romantic feelings never mingle

Still
Dreams speak to us

My ship sails across the sky
Where the sun, the moon and the stars shine together
Your smile pours down like dews of shooting stars
The trail of my ship turns into a beautiful road

People's dreams are transient
Even if they lose you when they wake up
People still continue to dream
Until the day they reach the realm of God's dreams

CHAPTER 2

The Sadness of the Firebird

火の鳥の悲しみの章

Phoenix changing its form

You are a wind
Without a form
You are a wind
Changing form
You are a wind
Till the end of the world
You are a wind
Until you are embraced

Reincarnation *ANSWER*

There was a man and a woman who fell in love and were united
The man was kind to the woman and her heart was full of happiness
As time passed, the man's love for the woman faded
She felt sad at heart though she pretended not to notice it
Before long, the man fell in love with another woman
He did not come home and the woman left on her own wept all night long
One rainy night
The man had an accident and lost his entire memory
The woman tried to bid farewell to him
But the man looked at her face and smiled
He had the same gentle gaze as when they first met each other

The man and woman fell in love again
The man was kind to the woman just like before and her heart was full of happiness
But after a while
The man began seeing another lover again and left the woman
One rainy night
The woman fell ill and was lying in a hospital bed
The man rushed to her side
The woman looked at the man and smiled
But the man did not appear before her after that

After many long years, they met again by chance and fell in love
The woman was kind to the man and the man's heart was full of joy
But in the course of time, the woman's heart had grown apart from him
The woman was hurt to see the man's sad face
Yet she had no idea why her love was fading
The woman fell in love with another man
She did not come home and the man left on his own wept all night long
One rainy night
The man fell ill and was lying in a hospital bed
But the woman never appeared before him again

Red String *VOICE*

Two souls were incarnated and became people
One as a man and the other as a woman
Then they met in this world and fell in love
They lived together for many years as a couple
And returned to a peaceful place

The two souls drifted down to this world again
One as a woman and the other as a man
But for some reason, the two souls kept missing each other
The two souls were never content in this world

To avoid making the same mistake as in their previous life
This time, they bound themselves with an invisible red string
(One that even they could not see...)
The two souls experienced various romances as they searched for the red string
But they still could not find their red string
In fact, they no longer knew what the red string meant
One night, many years after they came to this world
They murmured looking up at the sky
"Why were people born?"
Only their voices echoed in the stillness where stars and the moon did not shine
The two souls were very close to each other but deep darkness screened their faces
Yet the two souls knew for sure
They were the ones that had promised to search for one another

If you are uncertain about your love now
Close your eyes and listen to your love's voice
If that person's voice reaches deep inside your heart with a pleasant sensation
Then your choice must have been no mistake
But if you do not feel at ease even for one brief moment
It was probably the wrong choice
You were originally a soul that was neither a woman nor a man
When you fall in love, you are simply in love with that person's soul
You should not be misguided by a person's appearance nor by the game of love
The red string is the heart that is part of the soul and words to express the heart
And it exists in the tone of the voice conveying words from the heart

You *FOREVER II*

You who were once born inside a tree
And were called a fairy shining in a dense forest

You who were once born inside a rock
And lived through an astoundingly long lifetime

You who were once born inside a person
And your delicate heart trembled with joy and sorrow

You
Whose soul is transparent
You cannot be seen or touched
Nor possess even one fragment of your own heart
You are neither a woman nor a man
And in this world
You continue to change your form as in a dream

You were with a wind
You were with a flower
You were with a bird
And now you are with a person

Just where are you heading for
In your eternal life
Repeating life and death time and again?

Your burning passion of love
Your boundless affection
Your tears and laughter
Your heart's pain never healed

Death, as if to throw away a pebble
Will erase everything from you so easily

Ah, why were you born into this world?
Will you manage to find the answer in such a short time?

All your experiences will vanish upon death
You will lose every fragment of your memory
Your irreplaceable journey will return to nothingness due to death
Yet you have journeyed through life many times

Is your life meaningless?
Or is it meaningful?

On a very fine morning
You water the flowers as usual

Everything you care for in this world is what you once used to be

When you lie down on the ground
And look up at the sky full of stars

Whatever thought occurs to you is you yourself

You are beauty
You are affection
You are romance
You are solitude
You are sorrow
You are a dream
You are a star

You exist inside everything
You are the air itself never bound by anything

You are neither a man nor a woman
Neither a beast, a flower nor a tree
You are the transparent air and the brilliance of the cloudless heart
As you are the air, you should know

"There is something more important than gaining"

Whether it becomes yours
Or whether it does not
You know something invaluable exists in this universe

No matter
How faraway it is from you
And even if
It does not know you have life
You know something most wonderful
Exists for sure somewhere in this universe

When you were born in this world
There was nothing to worry about
Likewise, there is nothing to fear
Even before death

Because

You will only part from yourself and return to yourself
You are always yourself

Death *FUSION*

If you listen
To the sound of the wind
You will hear a dear melody

A soul on this planet
Becomes 'me' as a person, who loves 'you' as a soul
Some day my body will decay, so my soul cannot remain

Your eyes cannot see my image
Your ears cannot hear my voice
Your hands cannot touch my body

Though my soul has left my body
My soul is still beside you

Though my body has left this world
My image is still beside you

In your memory and in your mind forever

If you listen
To the sound of the wind
You will hear a dear melody

Flowing Clouds *EASY*

Things of perfection
Do they reign as rulers?
Or do they
Continue to change with us?

Clouds not changing shape
Flowers not withering away
Life without an end
If they are things of perfection
The word ‘rule’ would not have existed in this world to begin with

Winds flowing
Flowers withering away
Life leading to death
You live freely without been ruled by anyone

You are acting
Like a spoiled child
Asking for the impossible
Black things wanting white
White things wanting black

You were the one
Who had been ruling yourself

Things of perfection
Their beauty and preciousness of life
Can be perceived when you understand that you are your own ruler

It is near you
It is so unexplainably near you

Yet
Sorrow and joy
Are born in your heart
And begin to rule you
Then you begin to wish for things of perfection

When you call the name of God high up in heaven
Is the voice of your own heart reaching you?

You seek for perfection in things other than yourself
And wish to be led to more happiness

Though you know
Joy will disappear
When you gain eternal life

Clouds not changing shape
Flowers not withering away
Life never growing old

Do you know
The things of perfection you are seeking for
Exist within time that seems frozen?

When you simply accept
Joy, sorrow, fear and heartsease
You will not be ruled by anyone
Nor will you rule yourself

When you realise
That things of perfection
Are free like floating clouds
You will find a sweet sense of peace in your heart

Reason *LIGHT*

Flowers and trees, birds and beasts
All living things
Beings that must die to live together
You say
  People's lives are not much different as they live to survive
  What other cause can there be?

A long ago
The beginning of a late night
The moon shed a pale light in a cove and before the stars appeared
Two souls met on the shore
They were moved and thrilled by the soundless wind
It was love at first sight and they became one by loving each other

Their heartbeats overlapped and turned into a cosmic melody like God's breath
Stars began to move and illuminated the night sky

There was a time when nobody existed in the world
And there were only two souls that had hearts
No one else was there to call them gods
The beginning of a universe faraway
The man and woman fell in love as they searched for their other half

By the time the souls in love had begun to nurture affection
Countless men and women had come to exist in the world

Your joys and sorrows as a soul born as a woman
Are caused by me, who is your other half
I am the person whom you love the most and hate the most

Though I should know you better than anyone else
I have made you cry
Though I should love you more than anyone else
I have hurt you

Even so
Your teardrops will turn into beautiful stars
Illuminating the night sky, which will turn into people's hopes
Saying so, the god who is your other self disappeared

"We were born to live together"
The two souls' words dispersed into the wind of time

A wise person that you are says
People were born to learn about love

But there is also love that does not have to be learnt
If you encounter something captivating
Such excitement will become the twinkle of a star shining eternally in this universe
That very moment will become an eternal cosmic melody even after love fades away

A long time has passed since gods have been called 'people'
Men and women have been falling in love without reason
Passing love makes us forget even why we were born

In a world where the cosmic melody does not reach anyone
And even the sound of the rising sun is unheard
During a time when only human souls are wandering around

I smelt that familiar scent of the wind again
A soundless wind swaying the two souls
A quiet premonition of love turning into a wind shaking their hearts with excitement
The man embraced the woman, wishing this moment would continue forever

Before affection effaced romance
Another twinkling star was born in the night sky

CHAPTER 3

God and Prophets

神と預言者の章

Those with words of the void

Words are like clothes covering your naked body

They decorate you and protect you

If you can let go of words covered with ego

And express your heart honestly

Your heart will shine with God's dreams and be full of God's words

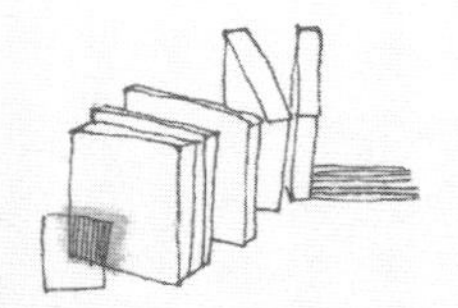

Words *ONE*

Words spoken with a seeming tongue are soliloquies even you cannot hear
Words spoken from your heart are gifts dedicated to God

Words learnt with your brain are your shadows not even to be remembered
Words learnt with your heart belong to God and you

If you want to perceive your own heart, you should look and listen with your heart

If you look with your heart, you can see everything
If you listen with your heart, you can hear everything

The rain muttering, the wind roaring
The seasons smiling, the sunlight's chorus
The stars singing and the horizon's sorrow

If you think with your heart, all is true

You said, "This world is miserable"
God did not hear your voice

You said, "There's no such thing as God"
God did not hear your voice

Lies told with your heart bring tears
Lies told with a seeming tongue create hatred

"I love you"
"I love you"
When words are written, only the words live and the heart dies

"I love you"
"I love you"
When words are spoken, only the words live and the heart dies

So you must look with your heart and listen with your heart

You cannot tell a lie before God
Just as you cannot change your face in the mirror

You have to perceive your heart
When you perceive your own heart, you will be able to encounter God

You can feel with your heart
That others are yourself and that you are God yourself

You can feel with your heart
That others are semblances of God and that the semblance of God is yourself

You said, "People can love without a cause"
God did not hear your voice

You said, "I will dedicate myself entirely to God"
God did not hear your voice

"Dedicate to God" is a phrase God hates the most
Because "God is dedicating to you"
(You are as one with others just as the others are as one with God)

You would "dedicate yourself"
Merely to a devil from God's point of view
(The devil will never become one with you)

All you have to dedicate to God are words your heart has learnt
(You are within God and God is within you)

Words bring two hearts together

You know and God knows
God knows and you know

You said, “I want to perceive God’s heart”
God also said, “I want to perceive your heart”

<table>
<tr><td>You look and</td><td>God looks</td><td></td></tr>
<tr><td></td><td>God looks</td><td>and you look</td></tr>
<tr><td>God listens and</td><td>you listen</td><td></td></tr>
<tr><td></td><td>You listen</td><td>and God listens</td></tr>
<tr><td>You talk and</td><td>God talks</td><td></td></tr>
<tr><td></td><td>God talks</td><td>and you talk</td></tr>
<tr><td>God talks and</td><td>you know</td><td></td></tr>
<tr><td></td><td>You talk</td><td>and God knows</td></tr>
</table>

Words learnt with your heart belong to you and God
Words spoken with your heart belong to God and you

You perceive God and God perceives you
Like air mixing and like lights blending

As if to exchange a kiss with God
You think with God’s heart and God talks through your body

My Soul *ANOTHER ONE*

My soul illuminates myself

My soul's shadow melts into the light and unites with myself
My soul woven and mixed with several lights and shadows
Loses even its identity

To look for the soul
Would deepen the sorrow
Desires are endless
Loneliness shuns love

Even a single flash of light
Hides itself in the looming time like the morning dew

I am my soul itself no matter who I am
You are my soul itself no matter who you are

You have hidden the truth within my soul
I have not found my own truth within my soul

Like the earth and the moon
Like the sun and the planets
I have a satellite that is my other self
I am by my side keeping a distance

My soul is my other self staring at my wandering self
Even when I forget myself
In joy, in sorrow and in anger
I am by my side
And watch myself quietly

Floating on a sea without waves
Playing with the waves, washed by the waves and sinking into the waves
Watching myself
At the same place in a different world where there is no existence
My soul is watching me

Some time ago
I was looking for God
Even though I could not find my own soul
I was wandering about in search for God who knew my soul

As if getting carried away with the burning passion of love
I was always in a dream

As if to collect the lights of numerous little stars
During a dark night, when the moon did not shine
My soul became obsessed with something
It was also trying to escape from something

Simply to go somewhere else
All along, I had simply wanted to go somewhere else

I was trying to escape from my own soul

I believed that waves would come from afar
But waves were the ripple of stagnant water
In the distant offing that I dreamt of
The quiet lull extended forever without surging

A place where the sea ends
Foams of waves washing against my feet
It is the only place where the sound of the sea can be heard

And the spot where I always used to be
Like the sand beaten by seawater
My soul is washed away by the waves splashing
Over and over again...

All along, I had simply wanted to go somewhere else

As there was no one who understood my soul
Not even myself...

Those who cannot even see their own soul
Those who cannot even hear the voice of their own soul
How could they understand others' souls?

Those who cannot even perceive their own soul
How could they perceive God's soul?

I was blind and did not know one single truth
I used to believe that only encountering the unknown
Would bring soul-shaking joy
I had even forgotten to pity the act of forsaking
Just like the repeating waves

God, now you are right here
Watching me silently
God, now you are right here
Listening to my soul's voice silently

When I know my own soul
I would be I and yet not I, nor even anything else
I see myself simply as one true soul

The moonbeam sheds light on the calm expanse of the ocean
Becoming a milestone for the ship carrying my soul

The blinking stars brimming in the sky
Are the myriad of twinkles I used to fantasize
When I scooped up with my hands and watched
The starlights floating on the sea
The same stars were shining on the water surface

What I have aspired
Spills over from my palms like an illusion
And disappears into the far distance

But now
The twinkles I have collected
Are turning into true radiance in my soul
Even illusions would change its image into true radiance

The truth is not made up of words
The truth does not have an image
The truth is a place where one's soul can return

It is the light of my own soul

If you understand your own soul
If you can see your soul's truth with your own soul
God is your other self

You no longer have to worship someone else as God
Nor do you have to fantasize God in your dream

If you can watch in silence
The image of your own soul

If you can listen in silence
To the voice of your own soul

Your other self will turn into God
Just as the wavelets washing against your feet
Are actually the ocean itself

Prophets *ANYONE*

When I was a child, I used to play card games with my uncle
At first, it was a guessing game of the picture card my uncle had in his hand
I had to guess the card hidden in my uncle's big hand without looking
Such as queen of diamonds or king of clubs
……It was like a clairvoyance game
Out of twenty games, I guessed right all twenty times
Soon I could tell which card my uncle would pick
Even a few seconds before he actually did
……A precognition game

Then next, I drew cards on a piece of paper
In the order my uncle would pick them up and put it on the table
Of course I turned it over so my uncle could not see it
My uncle lined up ten cards on the table
He seemed somewhat uncomfortable
We turned the paper up and found he had laid the cards
In exactly the same order as I had drawn
My uncle had meekly chosen the picture cards
That I had drawn almost unconsciously in random order
……It was neither a simple precognition game nor ESP

Now as an adult, whenever I feel God's miracles
I recall the card games I played as a child
And this is what I think
I may be leading a life according to God's will
Can anyone declare to God
That they have lived giving free rein to their heart's desires?

God's miracles visit me like a still wind without making it feel like a miracle
Just like air, it exists quite naturally in my body
It will not make me indebted or demand my gratitude
Nor will it hurt my pride or make me lose self-respect

You might be enraptured with self-praise for getting a chance and achieving success
Even then, God will never say, "I knew you would like it"
Or "Be grateful as you owe it to me"

You might be at a loss and shed tears of despair for making an unwise decision
Even then, God will never say, "It was for your own sake"
Or "It has given you a chance to recover your heart"

To live right by God's side
Is to be with life's entirety so naturally
That you do not see God
Nor feel the indications of God

Your joys and smiles
Your sorrow and weeping face
Your choices and chances
Your emotions and thoughts
And your encounters and partings
May all be just as God has intended

You felt no anxiety when you were born
For your soul already knew
You would lead a life with God

Not having to be afraid even of death
You will realise that people entrusted with God's words
Would never prophesy the future
Even if they could foresee a disaster
They would not proudly say, "My words are God's will"
God would never change time into words
Because God will change time into the void
And give us freedom
Even if we cannot play with time
We have a free space
In fact, in this space
We are so free that we would even forget God

Yet God will never forget you
And will speak to you over the course of time
This is the future told by God

If you want to discover God
Take a good look at your past and present
If you can accept your life and feel grateful to every fact
Then you will be able to find God
And understand
That nothing in your life was in vain

One day, you will realise that God is with you
And understand how important words are
This will also become your pure love for God

If you can love your own words
You also love God
If you hate your own words
You do not love God
Nor try to believe in God

By listening to your own words with your heart
You are listening to God's voice
By turning your emotions and thoughts into inaudible words of the heart
You are listening to God's voice

You are with God at every single moment
And one day, you will come to know
That everyone is God's prophet

A Mentor *GOD*

To encounter God
Even if it was only for a few brief seconds in a dream
Would be the most impressive experience remembered for the rest of one's life
God appeared quite clearly in my dream
Though I had never even heard God's voice
—It was not of my own accord but God who had let me experience such dream
It was such a special sensation for me
Like leaves hiding the branches as a tree grows
The image of God I saw in my dream
Has become more complicated as years go by
However, strangely enough
Whenever I try to recall God, my heart would become pure again
Whenever I imagine God, my heart forgets everything and I become true to myself
The God I saw in my dream a long ago taught me something so powerful
That cannot be explained well enough with words such as conscience, moral or love
It may be God's truth that no one has ever imagined before

One glorious day in spring
I met an old lady
She called me by my name
As if she had known me for a very long time even before I bowed
Her voice brought back dear memories and reached deep inside my heart
Even forgetting I was surprised that she knew my name
I was smiling like a child who had come back from a little adventure
And behaving bashfully in front of his mother

I visited her several times after that
Her words were always the same
“Honest young man, you must never forget gratitude and compassion”
To me she had simply turned into God that I saw in my dream

Then one day
A miracle suddenly came along
I saw the image of God once again
This time, God appeared not in my dream but occupied my entire field of vision
God just actually watched me without saying a word
The eyes of God tacitly taught me that my existence was nothingness
Time stopped and space became still in the eyes of God

Infinite space creating eternal time
Eternal time creating infinite space

Eternity is nothingness and nothingness continues to be eternity
God is eternity as well as nothingness

I came to know the universe with God beside me
It was neither a spiritual awakening nor the truth but simply what God was
God had become an existence far too big for me to perceive
Like eternity and nothingness

One summer afternoon, a few years later
I was sitting in front of her silenttly, listening to the sound of a wind-bell
Her presence before me was also unmistakably the very image of God

God is eternal and momentary
God is infinite and partial

The heart is momentary but it reaches eternity
The body is partial but it expands to infinity

A life is born and becomes eternity
A life dies and melts into infinity

Although God had been with me since long before I was born
I was not aware of God's existence
Just as we are not able to see our face with our eyes
God and I had continued to be as one
God is my eyes and my face is God's image itself

We can see our own face only in the mirror
But everyone can see the image of God reflected in their eyes
Yet it is more important to be grateful to God
And to be full of compassion for everything
Then people will become nothingness
Nothingness will reach infinity and eternity
And expand to the whole universe

As there is nothingness, eternal time continues
As there is nothingness, infinite space expands

Selflessness is to expand the self into gratitude and compassion
Selflessness is to assimilate the self with the universe
Selflessness is to integrate the self with the infinite and eternal God

In eternal time
In infinite space
Until the day you can identify yourself with God expanding endlessly
Nothingness will continue to exist

Till you realise that
Nothingness is not zero
But that nothingness is the infinite
And the very image of eternal God

Spiritual Awakening *BIRTH*

Those who wake up at night
And share deep sorrow and times gone by
Those who shut their eyes and cover their ears to the sound of the rising sun

Those who are excited over some hope still unperceived
And search for the voice of truth
Those who believe even in fraud as their aspirations have become strong cravings

Happiness and awakening lie in your unhesitating heart
Hesitation is indeed pain and sorrow itself

If you want to wipe away your sorrow
If you want to be spiritually awakened
Stop hesitating
As those who do not hesitate are the ones blessed with much happiness
And can be called spiritually awakened people

Like the moon, the earth and the sun
And the countless number of planets and comets

Which have left their tracks
In the endless time
And in the endless sky

In the infinite universe
Innumerable stars
Continue to create the rhythm of space-time without a moment's hesitation

That is Nature, in other words God
Nature's providence is indeed awakening itself

Therefore

When you are in love, you should love without hesitation
When you feel affection, you should feel without hesitation

Being in love without hesitation will make your pains disappear
Feeling affection without hesitation will open up a path of awakening

This is how
You will tread various paths of spiritual awakening

Like the sunlight pouring in
Like the wind sweeping the clouds away

Even if you are on the brink of death
You should leave no room for hesitation in your heart

Just like the universe
Just like nature's providence

Hoping there is not even one little sign of hesitation in your mind
And not even one trace of hesitation in your movements

Hoping you are far away from sorrow
Hoping you are very far away from hesitation

The unfinished universe you envisioned
When you were a child
In your mind itself

Hoping each thought
Occurring in your mind
Turns into a shining star

Hoping each and every movement
Of your mind and body
Is shared with Nature's providence

As spiritual awakening is the state of your unhesitating mind and body

There was a time
When you were spiritually awakened

At birth
Your first cry
Was the awakening of life bearing no hesitation

When you were born into this world
Your mind and body felt no hesitation
Hoping you will never hesitate and lead a life full of happiness

CHAPTER 4

The Beginning of Light and Darkness

光と闇の始まりの章

Why did angels become devils?

Those who reflect the light
Those who reveal their image
Innocently before me
Like the golden moon
Appearing in the pitch-dark sky at night

Are you aware of the agony
Of those who do not reflect the light
Whose hearts are merely a void
Like the dark sky at night?

God's Room *WHITE CANVAS*

You who are mortal
You who will eventually leave behind your shadow
Melt into the light and become an angel travelling from nothingness to infinity

You who are mortal
You who will eventually lose your shadow
Blend into the darkness and become a devil experiencing everlasting agony

Just as the body has a shadow, carnal desires create darkness

To have a shadow proves that you are alive
To have a dark side also proves that you are alive

Even though you are a devil, at first you were born as an angel

When you drew a picture in your heart just as you please
You drew joy and sorrow as well as your life

Whether to become an angel or a devil in this world again is all up to you

If you think that a plain canvas put in a frame
Is meaningless, try visiting God's room
Where white canvases are decorated all over the place

Whether you draw the blue sky or a green landscape
Shadows would be created in God's room anyhow

This was how the Creation was performed in the remote past
Plain canvases are the only things in this world that do not have shadows
It is the pure realm of God and what God looks like

God has no shadow and will never have a form

Even after you leave your shadow behind
Plain canvases will continue to appear in front of you
And
When you hold a paintbrush in your hand again
Will you be able to appreciate
The immeasurable preciousness of God's love
And God's irreplaceable love called freedom?

Kindness *COOL*

Your kindness
Is the other side of your utmost coldness
But you try not to notice it

Your coldness
Is the other side of your utmost kindness
But you try not to notice it

Your kindness
Is the other side of your utmost coldness
And devils know it

Your coldness
Is the other side of your utmost kindness
And angels know it

The more you become a person kind at heart
The more you understand cruel schemes

The more you become a person cruel at heart
The more you understand kind measures

To learn one kindness is to know one coldness
To know one coldness is to learn one kindness

Like sunshine casting dark shadows
You can see devils' images in kindness

Like dark shadows created by sunshine
You can see angels' images in coldness

You may be a kind person
But a devil also resides in you
You may be a cold person
But an angel also dwells within you

Your heart
As though it were God itself
Accepts both an angel and a devil at the same time
And
In your heart
Both an angel and a devil become you as one person

Shadows *WORDS*

You who reflect your heart in the light
As if to illuminate yourself in the light
The dazzling light making you shut your eyes
Creates a deep shadow by your feet
Your heart drowns in its darkness
And you will seek for light again
No matter how strong the light is, it cannot erase your shadow
All it does is to create deeper darkness

If you wish to turn into light
You have to know the pain of darkness

Kindness is with you like the shadow by your feet

If you are joy
The shadow is your pain

If you are an angel
The devil is your shadow

What can you see when you close your eyes?
What can you hear when you cover your ears?
What can you talk about when you shut your mouth?
In your heart
At the bottom of your heart like ocean depths where light cannot reach
Can you see the image of light shining through?
Can you hear the sound of light shining through?
Can you talk about the truth of light shining through?

When you realise
The image of light and the sound of light
Born from your heart is you yourself
You will know that light is born even from darkness

Light is not radiance
Light is the word and the very heart of God

Your body is God's heart
Your heart is God's words
Both light and shadow are God's embodiments
To be found where God's heart lies

The Light *UNIVERSE*

Before the universe was born
There was only eternal light
With no distinction of colours
With no intensity of radiance
Light spread evenly and endlessly forever

At one point
A dot of light began to brighten up as if it had burst forth
In amazing speed, its colour deepened and its brightness intensified

After a while
The dot of light with its powerful radiance was shining brilliantly all around
Light began to illuminate light by means of light
Light nearby became brighter in spite of itself
Light far away became darkness in spite of itself
Light began to create light and darkness by means of light

It turned out to be
The end of eternity
In other words, the beginning of the universe
It was also the beginning of light and darkness
Joy and sorrow, love and hatred
Good and evil, life and death, gods and devils

If the universe was born from nothingness
Nothingness is eternal harmony and God's perfection

If the universe is etched by space-time
Space-time is ruining of harmony and destruction of eternity

Time began to move
Space began to expand

Eternal harmony falling apart
Meant total disintegration of God's perfection

Before the universe began, there was only light and no darkness
It was
Light itself that had created darkness
Just one dot of intense light
Had turned the gentle shine of light into darkness

The appearance of a great light, i.e. a great God, called forth deep darkness

God of perfection
Why did you
Forsake eternal harmony to create this world?

If light is required to erase darkness
God, you should shine even brighter
But dazzling light only creates deeper darkness

Are you just going to continue shining
Until you find the answer?

When I woke up one morning
There was gentle sunlight
The light disappeared when I closed my eyes and I was surrounded by darkness again
In the darkness, I searched for the bright sunlight
Then behind my eyes
The spectrum of light began to shine
It was a soft radiance
In the darkness, the subdued light felt like a pleasant breeze
So as not to lose sight of the radiance
I kept on staring at the light with my eyes closed

When I opened my eyes again
The sun had set and darkness had surrounded the vicinity
But I could definitely see
The radiance of the light still shining gently in the darkness

The light in the darkness
Or the light that came to be called darkness was clearly visible

Darkness does not exist in light
Darkness does not exist in darkness
There is only a gentle light
What shuns the light is the blindness of the heart called 'ego'

I know that both light and darkness exist in my heart

God of perfection
You exist in light as well as in darkness

God of perfection
You created and fostered something irreplaceable from the eternal light
It is the greatest thing you have given us
Freedom is our own universe that God has given us
My soul is the universe itself, which is your love itself

The surprise, joy, agony and courage of loving
The sadness, justice, mistakes and happiness of loving

Even now you continue to shine gently into everything
Becoming the eternal harmony called love

We are with you in light and in darkness

At the end of the universe, there is no darkness
There is only light
Darkness is light without radiance
If you can see light shining in darkness
You will immediately realise
That the universe is alive in eternal harmony

A long time ago
The end and beginning of the universe
A particle of love turned into light and the rift of light became time and space

The double-sided space-time turned into a place for the universe to exist
Space-time became the theatre for God's words and words took on images

God's words began to bear shadows, words became egos and ran wild

Words were attracted to each other and words hurt each other
Pleasure and displeasure co-existed on the verge of desires
Those who lost love feared love and those who gave up love doubted love
They had merely restored their original state after gaining and losing love
But said the world had become an empty place not even worth existing

God settled down within serenity, hidden away from the words and glanced down
Then darkness surrounded the universe and all the radiance disappeared

The words that had lost their master searched for God
They sought after God without knowing they were part of God's words
At times they found comfort in what they loved, believing God was there
But those who had lost sight of true love could not find God

There is nothing that makes you happier than love or more bitter than love
As if they were seeking for God, the words sought after love and cursed love

God's tears became words and stars wandering in the dark universe again
God's heartbeat shook space-time and the universe began to move

Stars collided, words broke into pieces and God's tears turned into a galaxy
Which lit the universe with colourless light
Many of God's words disappeared from the world

The words only loved themselves and what they did not love were also themselves
They thought the world was brimming with innumerable words
It was because they did not know the truth about words

Just as God is a word, there used to be only one word in this time and space
It exists deep inside you, it is the source of emotions and thoughts
And it anchors egos like gravity
Love had turned into words, images and all creation

Now God's tears have turned into clouds and exist above me
I turn into a bird and soar high in the sky
I grab a piece from a cloud and toss it into my mouth
It tastes of hope and comfort

I can hear the winds singing
The clouds drift, the stars smile, the moon dances and love brims over
Innumerable words are born and truth pours down like rain
The galaxy is shining beautifully and has begun to add colours to the universe

CHAPTER 5

The End and Beginning of Eternity

永遠の終結と始まりの章

The happiness
Of being born from nothingness
And being able to return to nothingness

The joy
Of being born from love
And being able to return to love

One's life
Turns into a starlight
Shining forever

Creation of the Universe *FIRST LOVE*

In the beginning, there was love
There was only love in the nothingness with no space or time

Before you were born
Where no one could see
There was a place full of love
Inside your father's and mother's hearts

Before you were born in this world
There was your father and mother's love
Likewise, before the universe was born
There was God's love

If your life
Is the seed of a flower born in a life form called the universe
You are also the universe itself
Space and time are with you

Space
Is the embodiment of a life form called the universe
Time
Is the heartbeat of a life form called the universe

Just like your growth
Space is expanding
Just like your pulsation
Time is ticking away

Falling into a slumber in space
Falling asleep in time
For you to live
For you to die
Is one of the eternities in this space-time

Before anything existed, there was only love
You were born from love and will only return to love

Some day or another
The universe will also fall asleep
And return to where you are

You and the universe will become one again
In the nothingness where there is no space, time, light or sound

While listening to the quiet melody of love

Death of the Universe *NEW UNIVERSE*

Living beings

Have life and death
The universe also has life and death

The death of a living being

Is not that the cells comprising the body
Become zero
Upon death
The cells rot and decompose

Then the decomposed substances
Are incorporated into other living beings

What would the death of the universe be like?

At present, the universe

Is considered to be expanding
Will it continue to expand endlessly hereafter?
At one point will it start to contract
Or has it already begun to contract?

However, the death of the universe

Will come along for sure
Just as everything in this world is mortal

The death of the universe
Means the death of this space-time

Animals and plants

Repeat cell division from one little fertilised egg
They grow and then die
But will never contract to the size of a fertilised egg

If the death of space-time

Is to occur without the universe contracting
To the size of its beginning

Then one day

When time and space of this universe suddenly become still
That would be the death of the universe

Both life forms and substances
Will lose the time and place to exist in

In other words
Death will fall upon everything

If 'frozen space-time'

Is the death of the universe
Then the frozen space-time
Will fall apart in due time

What will remain afterwards?

God

Like one cell dividing into sixty trillion cells
Places a dream on one person to mature and to turn into a god

By giving each person a free will
God may be trying to create more gods

In order to create a divine universe expanding infinitely

When God Disappears *NAME*

“Physical matters are concentrated waves.” (Quantum theory of the 20th century)
“In the beginning was the word.” (The New Testament)

All creation in the world of nature has a name
Proving they were created by God
Words overflow from the heart and become ‘existences’
All creation is the picture envisioned in God’s mind that embodies God’s words

And we human beings
Have given names to everything we know in the world of nature
Why did God allow us to do so?
The answer must be

The clue to find out why we were born into this universe

Both in the past and present
We have given names to flowers and birds, and even to stars and galaxies
Moreover, we have given names to various natural phenomena
And knowingly or not, we call them ‘the rules of nature’

The rules of God also exist within our hearts as we share the heart of God

Human beings can give names to all creation, proving we share the heart of God
Our hearts are so close to God just as winds, seas, flowers, trees, birds and beasts are
And like all creation within the harmony of the universe
We human beings have been assigned important roles that only we can accomplish

Our ears are for listening to the voice of nature
Our mouth is for speaking the words of nature

We have to know those meanings
Because we human beings
Are the narrators of God's eternal heart

Some day or other
This universe will also come to an end
That is when God will disappear
But it will originate the creation of a new universe

In the heart of someone who has once heard God's voice
Who has spoken God's words
And
Who has been determined not to forget God's heart
Words will be born again and several universes will begin afresh on that day

All creation will be born in the heart of 'this person,' obtain words and become 'beings'

One day
We will give a name to ‘this person’
Who will be called ‘God’

As for
Where we are from and where we are heading for
It would require an even longer time to answer this question

However, there is something we must not forget

We must never forget
Why we gave this person the name ‘God’

Greenery bathing and shining in the sun
Birds flying about by instinct
The sun setting and the stars beginning to twinkle

Right now, everything in my field of vision is a part of nature
But I as a human being cannot become one with nature
Sometimes I live acting against nature or even frightened of nature

I ask myself, "Who am I?"
I ponder over who "I" am as the embodiment of God and a part of nature

It may seem as though a tiny little pea-sized mole on the tip of my finger
Is asking, "Who am I?"
God would probably reply
"You are my mole."
But I as the mole would say
"I am a mole and not you."
"I am a human and not God."

God is nature and nature is everything that exists
That is to say I am also part of God's embodiment
I believe I understand that

Jesus said
"Love thy neighbour."

One's self would expand by loving one's self and others alike
I loved my neighbours
I, who was once a mole, expanded my love to about the size of a fingertip

Then I asked
"Who am I ?"

God answered
"You are my fingertip."

"I am a fingertip and not God.
If I am God, please show me what God looks like."

God handed me a mirror and said
"If you want to see me, look at yourself and you will see my reflection."

My little fingertip was the only thing reflected in the mirror

"That is me"
Said God

"I am just a fingertip and definitely not you.
If you had not given me intellect
I could have identified with you as part of nature without worrying
Just like flowers, trees, birds and beasts.
Why did you give me the capacity to think like this?"

"You said just now that you are just a fingertip.
But I cannot imagine you to be thinking if you were merely a fingertip.
The fact that you are thinking right now means that I am thinking.
Though you may be just a fingertip, your heart is also my heart."

"Then please show me your brain."

"Even if I show you my brain, you probably would not believe it is an image of God."

"Then what shall I do?
You're not saying I should love the whole universe just as I love myself ?
It seems impossible in such a short life span."

"Gratitude sometimes surpasses the power of love
Because simply being grateful to the fact that you are alive may be more valuable
Than loving the entire world of nature."

"Is gratitude more valuable than love?"

"As you see, I am breathing now.
I do not have to think about it as I breathe.
My heart is beating.
I do not think about this, either.
When I walk, I do not think about taking a step with my left foot and then my right.
These are all my natural actions.
You have a nervous system, too.
It governs your natural actions so that you can live.
My consciousness is incessantly focusing on my body, in fact the entire nature.
The sky, clouds, earth, flowers, trees, birds, beasts and you people are all myself
And my consciousness itself."

"That may be so.
If you hadn't given me intellect
I could have assimilated with you unconditionally like the flowers
But how can I feel grateful to you
If to doubt God's existence as I do now
And to hurt other people or even to kill each other is also your consciousness?"

"For you to have doubts about me or to hurt and kill each other, all mean
You have doubts about yourself and that you would hurt and kill yourself.
Whether you have belief or doubt, kill each other or be on good terms
You are all with me as you are now.
As long as you are with me, you will not die in the true sense.
Cells will be reborn even after dying.
Even if you kill each other, new cells will be with me.
For me, you are my very cells repeating reproduction.
If you think of yourself as being one of my cells, you will be born again.
Real death will occur only when I die."

"Do you mean that my reincarnation won't come to an end until you die?"

"If you give a name to one of the cells, reincarnation will continue
But if you think you are me as God, you need not repeat reincarnation.
To put it more simply, it all depends on whether you can think of yourself as me."

"But to feel uncertain about it is also part of your thoughts, isn't it?"

"Your faith, however, is also my thought."

"Why do you have to be so winding?
Flowers, trees and birds don't face such trials.
You could have made us human beings like that.
Then nature might have become your peaceful divine world."

"Have you ever thought about freedom?
Freedom is to accept everything and to love everything
And freedom is to sacrifice everything and to love everything.
Freedom is not to live by being selective.
I am freedom itself.
I bring birth to everything and lose everything, even time and space, and life and death.
That is what I am."

"If every misfortune or disaster of this world
Is due to your free will
I can only think of them as God's whim.
If God's freedom is whimsical, I won't believe in God."

"You are free to think that way
And that is also one of my intentions.
There is one thing I want to say.
If freedom is eliminated, there will be no point in my existence.
If you do not dream of happiness, there would be no pain
But nor would you encounter joy.
You would not need God either.
If everything remains peaceful from the start
No one would have even thought of a need for God.
If God, which is nature and thus the universe, were to continue forever
It would be the same as if nothing had existed from the start.
God does not exist where there is no death."

"Do you mean you are going to die when the universe comes to an end?"

"Yes.
As the universe is indeed myself
Life and death is also myself."

"So will that be when all creation will end its reincarnation
And when the life of the phoenix repeating reincarnation will end as well?"

"Your reincarnation will continue."

"What?! You said that the lives of everything in the universe are one with God.
That means when you die, I won't have a place to live anymore."

"Everything including the flowers, trees, birds, beasts and countless stars
Will disappear with me, leaving you behind
But you will continue to exist as you know the truth."

"What does that mean?
It's hard to imagine life dwelling in a place where there's no time or space.
Or do you mean I'm going to become the time and space?"

"You have eyes to continue observing nature
Ears to continue listening to the sound of nature
And also a brain to develop wisdom and to keep memories.
You also have a heart to speak words.
In due time, having understood my heart, you might become the universe just like me.
You will create a free world within yourself just like I did
And realise that freedom is your own universe."

"Is that why you gave me this agony
That does not leave my thought even for a moment?"

"You people are seeds of flowers born in my universe.
You will soon gain true freedom
Which is so free that you will not even have to be bound by me who is God.
You simply have to envision a dream in your heart just as you please
Just as I did......"

There is something I have ponderd but got nowhere since I was a child

"Where did I come from and where am I heading for?"

Even now as an adult, my question remains the same
There was once a god who answered my question
He said he was the universe and nature

After a while, he left just as he had said
God disappeared and the universe ceased to exist
I was left all alone in a world without time or space

"Who am I?
Where did I come from and where should I go?"

I have come up with an answer
No, perhaps the answer is indeed myself
I said so as if to persuade myself

"I am free.
There is nothing to fear."

In the beginning was the word
Then freedom was created and the universe was born

My Universe *ANOTHER LOVE*

In this place and in this time
I could not meet you
There was the beginning, the end and eternity
You were in that place and in that time

However, that place and that time
Was a part of you given to me

You hid yourself in life and in death
In light and in darkness

Your birth was the beginning of that universe
Your death was the end of that universe

My place and my time
Must have been a part of you
But now you no longer exist

Romance could be the beginning of affection
Romance could also be the end of affection
Romance and affection, like the moon and sun
Continued to illuminate the entire soul

Romance is like egos competing
Everything that was sought for was romance
Affection is like egos trying to become one
Everything that was lost was affection

Darkness could be the beginning of light
Darkness could also be the end of light
Like light and darkness overlapping
Affection changed its images and you were always beside me

You were in my hope
    And in my despair

You were in my joy
    And in my sorrow

You were in my friends
    And in my enemies

You were in my parents
    And in my children

In stones, in water, in flowers, in winds
In smiles, in tears and in dreams
You were in everything
That I thought of, saw, heard and touched

You were like a dream ever sought after
You were like a dream that would never come true

You were the first thing to come in view at birth
You were the last thing to be felt at death

A long ago, no perhaps it is this very moment
I cannot remember
It was the moment when I no longer needed you
It was a place where you no longer needed yourself

Light bid farewell to darkness
Affection bid farewell to romance

Your birth was the beginning of that affection
Your death was the end of that affection

The time when affection bid farewell to affection
The place where I no longer needed myself

Joy and sorrow have become one
Benevolence and hatred have become one
Life and death have become one
Nothingness and infinity have become one

Can you imagine
The beginning of a new universe and the beginning of a new love?

The existence of a space-time where the future, past and present become one
Light and darkness become one
Love and affection become one

Now in this place and time that you no longer exist
I am standing alone

Who am I?
I try to envision my image
Faraway in my fading memories
I suddenly smelt that familiar scent of yours

I will try to envision myself just as I am
Just as you created that time and space

In this room, where you used to stay
I smelt the scent of lilies, which were your favorite flowers
But all I could see were shadows of confined space and seemingly stationary time

You follow the path of time and fill in the pages of life
You spend your whole lifetime to finish writing a book

Facing death, your heart wanders to and fro freely within your lifetime
And once again you encounter a book that is you

Whatever it may be
And even if it is something transient, disappearing when you do
You will come to know that it is something most irreplaceable

You are a book of the void

Your heart is boundless since your life is the void
Just as your heart was the very truth in your life
God's heart will continue to be true in this universe

You, as a part of the universe, share your heart and space-time with God

The void crosses over and turns into time
Time accumulates and turns into space

You may not know cosmic truth but you know entirely what your heart means

Love and joy, anger and sorrow, beauty and desire.........
These you understand without being taught from someone else

You had known such feelings even before you were born
You had a heart and words even before you had a body

All the words that occur to you are indeed God's image and the universe's truth
Your book of the void carries your heart's image and your truth

Your heart exists with time just like the invisible space of time
Your corporeity exists with space just like the transparent void

Your heart exists with God like time, your body exists with God like space

The body gets a heart and comes to life
Space gains time and turns into space-time

You share both God's heart like time and God's corporeity like the void

> The big wide world that opens up before you
> Represents all the words your heart has woven

God's mind lies even where this universe does not exist
The heart becomes words
Words become shapes

It begins from love and love becomes light
Light becomes time and space

Then it turns into the expansivity of the universe
Love has become the infinite extensity of the universe

God's heart changes its name to nature and becomes the image of all beings

God's love became the soul of all beings and engendered life
God turned love into shapes, which became the entire universe

Hence everything that exists is love

If all beings embody God's love
The gravitation of all beings is actually God's love

When you experience God's love
Your soul overlaps with God's heart even if only a little

At that very moment
Your words take shape
Your words create stories

Because your soul is also the fruit of God's love
Just like God, your words also turn into existences

Such splendor has never been seen before

The flesh and its desires cover up the splendor
Like light drawn by stellar gravitation, even love is distorted by fleshly desires

Flesh born from God's love covers up God's love
Yet such flesh is also created from God's words

Those not grateful to the flesh born from love are not grateful to God either

To know love, you lose love
To know happiness, you lose happiness

You may know about being loved but not about not being loved
You may experience happiness but not the state of unhappiness

These states of the mind are far from love

A place far away from love is darkness
Darkness is not found in sadness and pain
It is found in hearts without compassion

If you think light is only the beautiful radiance, you are a person of darkness
If you think love is only the pure and right mindset, you are a person of darkness

Nature teaches us those things

To reflect God's love in your soul, your love has to be scarred
As if to grind diamonds, your love has to get scarred countless times

When you know God's love
Your words turn into existences

God's love has gravitation
That attracts words
And words turn into existences

EPILOGUE

The Fleeting yet Beautiful Truth of Abstruseness

難解なるものの儚くも美しい真理の章

Light and darkness intersecting

Time ticking away

All existence turning into memories

Left behind in space-time

The future is the shadows of existences yet to come

The shadow of the moon yet to shine

The future not reaching my memory

Is the daytime moon yet to shine

Existing in the same space-time as I do

Where the Heart Returns *UTOPIA*

"Why was I born?"
You asked this to yourself many times when you were a child
You got older without finding the answer
Searching only for joy and avoiding pain just like others

As if you were a slave controlled by endless desires
Your heart never found peace

As if you were a runner who did not know his goal
You continue running single-mindedly like clock hands spinning on a dial

Now you find yourself thinking that life is like a competition
You have found joy in being superior and dismay in being inferior to others

You cannot be happy on your own and always need someone to compare with
You can find happiness or unhappiness only outside yourself and not within

Like water poured into a bottomless cup, your feelings pass through your heart
As your heart remains immature, you wander through life like a blind traveler
When you hear the footsteps of death
The thought of death causes ceaseless anxiety as you cannot see the goal

Then you think about the meaning of life again

Life is to look for the goal before death arrives
Life's destination is not death but to reach your heart's home

Even if you lose something precious
You will know that you have not lost anything by putting your heart there

Even if you are surrounded by darkness
By putting your heart there, you will know that there is no such darkness

Everyone was born in this world and incarnated in order to reach that place
All emotions connected to the body help your heart find that place

One snowy morning
You saw an old lady in the blizzard

"Where on earth are you heading for in such heavy snow
When it is so cold and the visibility is so low?"
"I'm not heading anywhere, I'm just trying to go back."

She said with a voice full of warmth that I was the one who was lost

Knowing the pathway to return makes life into a happy journey
Other pathways turns life into a never-ending wandering around

Knowing where the heart returns turns death into a peaceful sleep
Not knowing where the heart returns turns death into unacceptable fear

My soul had searched for a place to return in the heart for so long
But my heart had not realized it and I strived to reach for happiness far away

Just as every emotion returns to the heart wherever it has been before
No matter how many times you go through different reincarnations
Your heart is the only place for your soul to return

The Heart's Free Rein *SANCTUARY*

I stand where there is a sweeping vista and throw away fake clothes
My heart sings as the blowing wind and the warm sunlight touch my skin

A wanderer going to and fro between freedom and restraints
Whose face is smiling and crying at the same time

Now at last you have found a home to return to

You have closed your eyes at reality as if to avoid the spring dust
Now you are excited to hear the spring breeze sing and the trees and grasses whistle

You have hid yourself in the shade, deploring the glaze of the scorching sun
Now you are thrilled by winter's snow-covered tranquility and a shadowless world

A long time ago, you whom I loved became the cause of my heart's pain
I have been crossing seas of illusion and calling at ports in mirages ever since
Wavering between illusion and reality, thinking ideals were merely passing dreams

I encountered and parted with many people, I laughed and cried many times
I met kind people and cold people
I met wise people and foolish people
I lied and others lied to me, and I told the truth and listened to the truth

However, my hands were colder than anyone else's
They turned even colder whenever I felt someone's heart
It was because I was lying to myself

I tried to hate important things and tried to love unimportant things
I thought of the past as I looked at the future and was selfish but referred to kindness
One night in the deep darkness after the storm, I met you when you were still young
My eyes flooded with tears and my heart was full of joy and love

The clear autumn sky is blue painted on white, reflecting the shining sea and the mist
My frosty breath, the cold wind and an exciting premoution of happiness

How happy I would be to embrace you as if to embrace the sky
How happy I would be to kiss you as if to kiss the sky

Now I stand on the road going west, mesmerized by the beauty of the sky at dusk
With vermillion tint and silhouetted trees, and everything soon melts into the night

This road leads to the darkness of night
This heart ends up in the tranquility of death
No, this road actually leads to you, who has a beautiful heart like dusk
This road continues deep inside my heart as it is only for me and only I know it

I thought you created a complete universe bestowed with an incomplete heart
But now I understand
Incompleteness has actually been your dream
God's freedom exists only in things beyond God's control

I can hear the wind, I can smell the sunlight and I can hear your voice

"You do not obey anyone or rather cannot obey.
Your dreams and despair is a world I have not yet seen.
You are what I have created yet you do not belong to anyone.
Reined neither by desire nor conscience, where did you get that freedom from?"

I unwittingly start dashing straight towards a place beyond this road
I am taking this road to go and see you
I am following this road to see you once again

The Heart *GOD*

The heart that hurts your feelings is you yourself
The heart that makes you wild with joy is you yourself

The heart hides in your body and treats you as it pleases
You apply the word 'soul ' to the heart and the part of yourself beyond your control

You blame your sufferings on someone else
But it is usually nothing more than your own heart that makes you suffer
You say that you owe your happiness to someone else
But it is always nothing more than your own heart that brings you happiness

You may think that the heart is born from your body and exists with the body
However, the heart is neither born from the body nor attached to the body

الجمال Красота Schönheit 美しさ Làm đẹp Ομορφιά 아름다움 יופי
زیبایی Kagandahan Uzuri Գեղեցկություն Beauty

حزن Печаль 안타까움 Tristezza Θλίψη עצבות غمگینی Lungkot Huzuni
悲情 Nỗi buồn 切なさ Տխրություն Tristețe Sadness

أمل Надежда 희망 Hoffnung Espoir Ελπίδα מקווה امید Pag-asa Matumaini
希望 Esperança Hope

Though you may not know how to call these sensibilities, you know the meanings
You can make distinctions between beauty and ugliness without being taught
Likewise, you know the meanings of sadness and hope right from the beginning

Because your heart has existed since before your birth
All you are doing is to feel your heart

The heart has existed since long before the Creation

Before this universe was born, several hearts were engendered
Everlasting time seemed to pass by without any of the hearts taking on form

Then God gave images to the hearts
Love first became a dot of light in the nothingness and it's shadow became darkness

Innumerable joys and sorrows burst out from one dot in the nothingness
Sound was born, time came into being, quietness appeared and the void was born
On that moment, the universe was created and life and death came about

In time, myriad of hearts transformed into all creation and came to life
The myriad of hearts hid themselves in words and became seeds of life

Just as every word exists in God's heart, every aspect of God exists in this world
Nothingness and infinity, life and death, light and darkness, the past and present, the beginning and end, and love and hate
Contradictory words born from one heart fly off in infinite directions like the stars

Truth changes its answers like illusions and the universe is full of dream-like puzzles
As soon as you think you have felt God, God changes its images into you
Not knowing how to search for God, you end up worshiping an idol of God

Your soul and your own self that are beyond control are indeed the heart of God
What no one can control is God and your heart

The God you have constantly searched for is nothing else but you yourself

You should think that your heart belongs to God
You should think that your joy, sorrow, kindness, tears
And your entire self belong to God
When you think of God, you exist in all creation

You are freedom itself and you are the God in the dream God has dreamt

You fly as a bird, travel the seasons as a wind, course the universe as a meteor
And then fall asleep quietly, cradled in the heart of your loved one

The Road *MY HEART*

Just as stars are born in the night sky, your road is born in this world
Just as roads are formed on land by cutting across the wilderness
Your road is created as you go through your life

There are sea routes on the oceans and air routes in the skies
However, you always walk with your own feet
At times, you stand motionless and be on the verge of desperation
At other times, you dash through like the wind and go into raptures

When you entered this world, you stood at the beginning of a road
When you disappear from the world, you will stand at the end of the road

There is a beginning and an end, and you are the only one who has trod this road

I have always been looking far down the road
Without looking at the reality in front of me
I was looking miles ahead over your shoulders

When a light is cast in front of me, a shadow is created behind me
I thought hope existed only in the future and only fragmeuts of dreams existed here
I always longed for tomorrow and overlooked the happiness from each step I took

I always forgave myself but did not forgive others
My heart did not look at myself but always looked at the hearts of others
Doubt passed through me and it remained in other people's hearts

Beauty is the seed of desire created by God
Ugliness is despair generated from people's hearts

You may be beautiful
But has not your heart decorated with false words decayed?
Where do you clean off bad odor that is scentless and dirt that is invisible?

When you speak to others with heartless words, they respond with empty words
When you speak to them with a truthful heart, they respond with truthful hearts

When you speak to your own heart with truthful words, how would it respond?
Is conscience a part of God?
Or is it merely my arbitrary assumption?

Can my conscience substitute the conscience of all things?
Can my god become God of all things?

I have questioned the part of me that exists in your heart
But it was neither my true self nor my conscience

My loved one
How happy I would be to share our true hearts and to walk along this road together!

Nevertheless, I am the only one that can walk along my road
Just as I cannot lead your life
No matter how much I love you

A beautiful wind does not have an image
It is bestowed on fragrant spring grass, falling autumn leaves and your waving black hair

Images of beauty that can be seen and beauty that can never be seen
And images of a gentle heart and a strong heart are bestowed on all things

Ginko leaves are hovering about in the wind
Winter is almost here

Sunlight filtering through the trees are warm like God's kiss
I close my eyes and embrace your kindness

Light exists not far down the road but right beside me

Sweet Illusions *ISOLATION*

When you were a child
And visualized your thoughts
The wind was clear, the sky was high and the sun was shining
Life was full of hope and your life was like a never-ending straight road

Your heart, however, is now making an endless journey

Those who realize their dreams
Lose dreams

Those who cannot accomplish their dreams
Find dreams

The love and passion for what you sought after disappear with the dreams
You take the world you dreamt of for granted and set sail on a new ship unnoticed

You stand on the seashore and dream about a faraway place on the ocean
When waves flow in and splash your feet, you wipe it offhandedly

Even though your dream has come your way and touched your body
You are not aware of it nor do you feel any joy

The drops of water you wiped away are part of the ocean you have dreamed of
But you try not to realize it

Even though hope should dwell within your heart
You are always dreaming far away from your heart

There are no days of rest and quiet in the endless repetition of illusions
A life without an end is to wander about forever

It is only death that makes life into a journey with an end

Time eventually lures the soul sent into the bustling world to a place beyond serenity

Have you gone through life in order to return to nothingness?
Where are the dreams you have envisioned in your life now?

As your consciousness fades away
Fragments of the vanished past bring back memories and start to shine like jewels
They soon turn into teardrops and cleanse your soul

Having left behind irreplaceable things, could you have become someone else's dream?
The warm and endearing feeling of being loved well up and you cry all on your own

You dream your last dream
To see the happy smiles of those you have sought for and those who have loved you

You have always been lonely but the peacefulness you have been seeking for
Now lies within your heart in your fond memories of everyday life

As in a Dream *THE DISAPPEARING PENINSULAR*

One sunny day in autumn
She showed him to a place where plants and trees had taken root in the water
He walked along a footway of trees built above the water
It had looked quite different from a distance and he realized it was not a place for people
Many days were cold even in summer and flowers bloomed only for a short while
In winter, everything got covered in white

She says that in her distant memory, she sees him standing in a field of water
Getting a bit shy, he gives over his soul's past to her crystal-clear eyes
The water surface reflects the sunlight and shimmers like a kaleidoscope

Wild birds sing, an erne flies off like an arrow and the sun sets soon after
He rubs his hands that have turned cold and prepares to leave
The veil of night is just around the corner
Thinking about a warm room and a warm meal, he takes her hands
His hands were cold but they felt warm to her
Time passes by as fast as light and hearts are left in the past

Everyone who has grown old says that life is long and yet short
Time passes
Many pasts sway to and fro in our memories like boats drifting on the river of time
Those who have turned their backs on death board an abandoned ship

They linger in the past and wander on the brink of desires like shadowless apparitions
Love used to dwell in the dazzling light
Love now lies in the closed darkness

People gather the meaning of life through their limited encounters
All encounters come out of the blue
But they are inevitable quirks of fate
There are as many stories as the number and the order of encounters

Like the wind swaying and ruffling the water surface
You try to give our fates some surprises
To be alive is to think of you and to adore you

To live in the eternal passage of time is only one brief moment
It is like a drop of rain that no one talks about
Like an illusion wavering between nothingness and endlessness
The heart vanishes like a transient dream

One stormy night in summer
They were in a room by the sea
She was hurt and there was an invisible wall between them
As if to cut through the silence, white lightening struck the night sky
Though scared amid peals of thunder, she said the glittering blue sea was beautiful
When he opened the window, damp wind blew in and moistened her cheeks
He embraced her and felt as if time would continue forever

My loved one, to whom does your heart belong?

A sea bird hovers above this peninsular that will disappear in time
You who are far away
Will you come to know that people used to live here
Experiencing several joys and griefs?

The sun setting in the marshes and the moon rising
The beautiful evening glow dyeing the western sky and the twinkling stars
This is where night and day overlap, and where darkness and light cross

I doze off in the northerly wind and then from somewhere, I hear your voice
When I kiss the cold sky
God's sigh becomes the wind
My heart starts to play God's words like the leaves of trees dancing in the air

Multiverse *SYNCHRONICITY*

Natural science is based on analyzing information obtained through man's five senses
It has become everyone's common sense and is called 'the truth'

Birds and beasts would look at the truth of the world quite differently than us
How is the world reflected in the minds
Of those who have senses that by far surpass humans' five senses?
How is the world regarded
By those who have intelligence that are by far superior than human intelligence?
For them, does our wisdom seem poor and inferior
Just like how we look at the beasts?

The truth that we know of is only the truth for humans

If one day, once-in-a-lifetime coincidences begin to occur repeatedly
And the world in your imagination unfolds before your eyes
Would you still think
That the coincidences in our world are merely coincidences?

You open an old album and recall sweet memories of your first love
A few minutes later, you hear a knock and see your first love standing by the door
He saw you in his dream last night and has come to see you after tens of years

Let's say you set out on a journey
You meet a good person by chance and have a nice time together
A few months later, you go on another journey
You meet another good person and spend a happy time
And also in your next journey and in the following journey...
As a child, losing your mother from a brain disease, you had mental issues
And did not have a friend
Now on each journey, you make up for your past by spending a happy fulfilling time

The people you met, though, had something in common, which you were unaware of
It was that they all died soon after they met you
They were all suffering from brain cancer and had very short time to live

One sunny afternoon
You are reading a book in the park and see a soap bubble floating in the air
Thirty minutes later, you finish reading
And see the same bubble floating in front of you as though it has stopped in mid air
When you stare at the bubble
It drifts away until it disappears into the darkness of dusk
The next day at the library, you pick up a book lying on the floor
And see a picture exactly like the bubble you have seen
It says, "Third Day of the Creation drawn by Hieronymus Bosch"

From that day onwards, whenever you experience synchronicity
You remember the bubble that does not pop

You can identify a bubble in the sunny sky
But not in the darkness of night
For a bubble does not emit light but only reflects light
If your heart is clear like the sky and harbour only pure thoughts
Everyone will be able to see what you are thinking
If your heart is full of darkness and holds deep dark thoughts
No one will see what you are thinking

You who cannot even see your own image in the darkness
Will come to know that only your conscious mind is the way to prove yourself
Dispelling darkness, your heart brims with light and clear thoughts will reflect light
Like a bubble that shows its image when it shines in sunlight
Your thoughts turn into images and shapes when reflected in the light of God
Your thoughts will come to exist when they are illuminated by God's love

Like a bubble appearing when light is reflected, God's love created your image
Everything in our world lies in God's love
Because everything that comes into view reflects God's light

Even so, you still think that everything in the world exists in space-time
That time shifts from the past to the future and space is time overlapping

However, both time and space are like mirrors reflecting things that exist
As can your thoughts go freely to the future or the past
As can your thoughts reach the end of the universe

Everything that exists has neither a past or a future nor nothingness or being
Everything is the image of the conscious mind reflected in the mirror of space-time
Just as mirrors do not function as a mirror where there is no light
Space-time cannot become space-time without God's love

All space-time exists in this radiance that is like a blink of an eye
Beyond space-time
Lies God's infinite mind that is so clear as to be called nothingness

『神のくちづけ』刊行によせて

原　麻美子

最初の作品『神のみる夢』が出版された時、なぜ、このような感銘を与える本が、さらさらと書けてしまうのか分からなかった。それほど著者は、いつも自然体で親しみやすかったからだ。

当時、タイトルをみて「神様でも夢をみるのだろうか」と不思議に思った。誰もが現実だと思っているこの世界は、自分という主人公が思い描くストーリーを、映画にしたようなもので、実はイリュージョンだったのだ。

今回の『神のくちづけ』は、タイトルそのものが謎めいていると思う。著者は人が恋をするのは、相手の中に神を求めているから。神への憧れが恋心を生むと説明している。恋多き人にはそういう理由があったのだ。しかし、いつかは恋から醒め、あれは幻だったと気づく時がくる。すると、今度はもっと遠くへ遠くへと探しに行く。ところが大海原の彼方まで辿り着いても見つからない。そして、真理を探究する長い旅から戻った時、同じ海水が打ち寄せる足元、実は自分自身がそうだったと初めて発見するのだと語っている。
『神のくちづけ』はファンタジックで壮大な宇宙の果てしない物語。「人は何処からきて、何処へいくのか」という永遠のテーマに対して、人間の存在の真実を解き明かした作品だと思う。あまりにも美しい言葉にすっかり引き込まれてしまい、内容を頭で考えようとすればするほど、分からなくなっていく。これは直観的に感じとる本ではないだろうか。答えは元々、私たちの深い意識の中で、眠り続けているだけなのかもしれない。そっと扉を開ければ一筋の光が差し込み、小さな目覚めがはじまるようにも思える。その光が『神のくちづけ』であり、心の奥から感動の波紋を呼び起こすのである。

「あなたは神がみる夢の中の神そのものなのだ」。そう語る合田氏の若々しく快活な印象は以前と変わらない。今も、人々に生きる智恵を示し続けている。

On the Publication of *The Kiss of God*

Mamiko Hara

When I read Mr. Yasuhiro Goda's first book *The Dreams of God*, I did not understand how the author could write such inspirational poems so smoothly. It was because he always had a very relaxed, open and friendly attitude.

When I first saw tht title, I wondered whether God had dreams. Now I have come to understand that the world regarded as reality is actually an illusion like a film, in which stories that we, as the main character, visualize are portrayed.

The title of the author's new book *The Kiss of God* is somewhat cryptic. He explains that people fall in love because they seek for God within the person they love and that the adoration for God creates the feeling of love. It may be that people who constantly fall in love do so for this very reason. However, one day, we fall out of love and realize that it was nothing but an illusion. Then we start searching even further away. Even when we reach the oceans far in the distance, we still cannot find what we have been looking for. Eventually, we return from a long journey in search of truth and notice that the same seawater is lapping our feet. Then we understand for the first time that we are the ones that actually embody the truth.

The Kiss of God emcompasses a neverending story about the fanastic and spectacular universe. I think it is a work that gives us insight into the existence of mankind that starts from the eternal question of "Where do people come from and head for?" I was totally mesmerized by the beautiful words and the more I tried to analyze the poems with my head, the more I got confused. Therefore I think this is a book to be read intuitively. The answer may already lie somewhere deep inside our consciousness. When we quietly open a door, a ray of light might shine inside and stir us from our sleep. *The Kiss of God* is the ray of light that causes repercussions of sensations deep inside our hearts.

"You are indeed God in God's dream," says Mr. Goda, who has a youthful and active impression as always, and he continues to provide inspirations for our lives.

神のくちづけ

2017年1月28日　第1刷発行

著者　合田和厚

発行所　株式会社マインドカルチャーセンター
〒145-0071　東京都大田区田園調布2-8-13-101
電話　03（3721）6365
振替　00130-9-137973
印刷・製本　株式会社東京印書館
英訳　角田美知代
NDC920

Published by Mind Culture Center Co., Ltd. Printed in Japan
ISBN978-4-944017-07-2
乱丁本・落丁本は小社負担でおとりかえいたします。